Praise for Lydia Millet

"[Lydia] Millet has perfected charged, science-based prose that takes a surgeon's loupe to how people interact with nature."
—L.A. Taggart, *San Francisco Chronicle*

"Millet is one of the most fascinating novelists working."
—*Wall Street Journal Magazine*

"Iridescent prose." —Katie O'Reilly, *Sierra*

"There is something undeniably compelling about Millet's writing, particularly her shrewd examination of human relationships"
—Michael Delgado, *Literary Review*

"*Dinosaurs* is a subtle, character-driven story about modern life and how to be a good person [that] considers big questions. [Millet] effortlessly puts the small dramas of her character's lives into wider context." —Melinda Copp, *Post and Courier*

"This gentle, redemptive novel follows a damaged, trusting man as he heals through human connection and requited love. . . . [I]t leaves a warm afterglow and an optimism that lingers."
—Sally Morris, *Daily Mail*

DINOSAURS

DINOSAURS

A Novel

LYDIA MILLET

W. W. NORTON & COMPANY
Celebrating a Century of Independent Publishing

The author wishes to thank Jenny Offill, Saralaine Millet, and Kate Bernheimer for their editorial suggestions, as well as all those at Norton who helped to make this book and bring it to readers: Tom Mayer, Elizabeth Riley, Amy Robbins, Anna Oler, Don Rifkin, Rebecca Homiski, Nneoma Amadi-obi, Ingsu Liu, and Steve Colca.

For information about special discounts for bulk purchases, please contact W. W. Norton Special Sales at specialsales@wwnorton.com or 800-233-4830

Manufacturing by Lakeside Book Company
Book design by Marysarah Quinn
Production manager: Anna Oler

Library of Congress Control Number: 2022027162

ISBN 978-1-324-06612-5 pbk.

W. W. Norton & Company, Inc.
500 Fifth Avenue, New York, N.Y. 10110
www.wwnorton.com

W. W. Norton & Company Ltd.
15 Carlisle Street, London W1D 3BS

1 2 3 4 5 6 7 8 9 0

DINOSAURS

MOURNING

WHEN HE DECIDED to leave New York, he chose Arizona because of some drone footage he'd seen. It wove through the canyons of red-rock mountain foothills, over sage-green scrub and towering cacti with their arms outstretched. Then up into the higher elevations, where there were forests of ponderosa pine.

Sky islands, was what they called those desert mountains.

Gil was keenly aware, watching the video, that he himself would never glide over the rolling landscape with that hypnotic steadiness. Would never coast over trees as the metal bird did— close enough to see the clusters of green needles on the pine boughs dip and sway in the wind.

He was also aware of the artifice of the soaring choral music the footage was set to. No landscape came with that.

Still it captured him. The desert had an alien beauty that

seemed as different as you could get, within the lower forty-eight. The opposite of Manhattan.

He recognized the pattern. He went to new places because they weren't the same as the old ones.

But he wanted to feel the distance in his bones and skin, the ground beneath his feet. Not step onto a plane and land in five hours after a whiskey and a nap.

And not drive, either, with the speed and convenience cars gave you.

He wasn't looking for easy. He had nowhere to be and no one who needed him.

On hiking websites he researched what he should carry, the weight of camping gear and water and food. He plotted his route painstakingly, spreading out paper maps on his kitchen table, checking each segment against local data from Google. The route that cut sharply south, because of the cold that would descend before too long, then straight west, along the bottom of the country from Georgia to Louisiana, through Texas and New Mexico.

Not much longer than the Appalachian Trail. Which people hiked, from beginning to end, every year. But harder in several details, since the asphalt arteries of the nation weren't designed for feet.

Then he'd sold his loft in the Flatiron District. Bought a house in Phoenix sight unseen, save for virtual tours and curated, artfully lit photos. Packed up his possessions and had movers come and take them there.

The long walk lasted for almost five months. He rested whenever his legs or back were aching—an ache that got less acute after the first couple of weeks—and stayed in motels when he could find them. The farther west he went, the greater the distances from one to the next. In Texas, even at a pace of twenty-five miles a day, sometimes four days passed between gas stations. And more than a week between motels. He had to carry a lot more water then. Ration it carefully.

Besides the weight of water and the cold, bathroom and shower availability were his most serious problems. He got rank when he had to camp out for too long—he knew this rationally, though he was mostly immune to the odor—and sometimes a front-desk clerk gave him attitude. At first glance, he looked and smelled homeless.

But his credit checked out and he cleaned up nicely.

On the walk, time moved so slowly that he ceased to measure it. It could be relentless in its tedium.

Other times the slowness seemed like grace.

At those moments, he looked back on the measured days and hours of his life in the city—its boxes and rows, its tidy compartments—and came to believe that version of time was the false one.

A grid designed, like the city itself, to keep everyone in their assigned seats.

FOR WEEKS AFTER he moved into his new house, the glass one next door was still up for sale. Curious, he'd taken a break from arranging furniture to go to a showing.

It was a mid-century-modern masterpiece, the real estate agent boasted.

Though technically, built in the nineties.

From his place you could see most of its interior, except for the bedrooms and bathrooms. It was laid out in an open plan: entry, living area, dining area and kitchen. On the side facing his house, the wall was one long stretch of glass.

On the other side, in the bedrooms, there were regular picture windows. He was the only neighbor with a view of the glass-walled stage.

He'd asked himself who would choose to live there. On display.

But he was still getting used to the air and silence of his house—older than the glass one, with such spacious rooms and high ceilings that he thought of it as a castle—when a family of four took up residence there.

A husband, a wife, a girl, and a boy.

He lived by himself. So it was hard not to look at them. At first they seemed like a group of mannequins to him, in a high-end department store window.

Say Bloomingdale's. Or Saks.

MAYBE PRIVACY JUST MATTERED LESS to the family, he thought, than what you could see from within. The glass wall was equipped with remote-controlled screens—the realtor had shown him their quiet movement—that rolled down to keep out the heat, protecting the house from the desert summer. At the end of a hot day you could press a button, if you liked, and raise the screens again.

That way you could watch the sun rise in the morning. And in the evening, from the windows in the west-facing bedrooms, you could watch the sun set.

At night the indoor lights made the glass house into an even brighter theater, its colors and figures vibrant against the surrounding dark.

The parents were slightly younger than he was, he guessed. Late thirties or early forties, possibly. The woman was blond and wore her hair up in an elegant roll when she went out, taking it down with one deft hand at the back of her neck when she came in again. The man was tall and had chiseled features, a sweep of black hair on his high forehead, olive skin.

The little boy was his father in miniature, and the teenage girl resembled her blond mother.

ONE AFTERNOON HE NOTICED the wife moving around in the kitchen—it was a cloudy day and the screens had been raised. When he sat down to read a book in his favorite armchair, and looked up from the page, he could glance through a gap in the drapes of the window beside it and see the full sweep of the open plan.

Idly he watched her stretch out the end of a roll of silver foil, rip off a neat sheet. She covered something in the foil, then gestured to the children—the boy, who sat building Legos at the dining-room table, and the girl, who roused herself from a couch in front of the TV.

The three of them went out their front door, the wife carrying her foil-wrapped plate, the children lagging.

They walked down to the sidewalk and turned toward his own front yard. Then up his front walkway.

For a second he felt trapped. Not ready for a meeting.

He looked down at his feet: one sock had a hole at the big toe.

But they had to know he was home—his car was parked in the driveway. If his car was here, he was here. Phoenix was built for cars, like LA. You barely moved without them.

Buying a car had been his first act, when he arrived. In New York he'd never needed to own one.

They rang the doorbell, so he shoved on his shoes and went to the entryway. On the screen of the security console he could see them—the wife smiling up at him, the tops of the children's heads behind her, indistinct.

Damn, was his thought, and he felt his pulse quicken. Alarm, but also a sliver of anticipation: it had been a dull sequence of days.

And opened the door.

The wife, who was even more elegant up close, said what friendly neighbors said in TV shows from the fifties.

It was a peach pie. She hoped he liked it—she was a mediocre cook, but when it came to baking you just followed the recipes.

Plus her daughter had helped. She liked to make desserts.

Her name was Ardis. The children were Clem and Tom.

Gil said his own name and stiffly shook hands all round, stooping to reach the children. They were awkward. Not used to handshaking. It wasn't a thing, he realized, with kids.

Maybe you weren't supposed to shake hands with them, these days.

Then he accepted the pie. Said thank you and stood there holding it. A man who had received an offering.

Was he required to ask them in? He thought not. The kids wouldn't want to hang around.

"We won't keep you," said Ardis.

He was supposed to utter a protest, manners dictated. But his lips didn't move.

"Thank you again," he said finally. "It looks delicious. This is very kind. It should have been the other way around—I should have thought of it myself. Brought you flowers, or something. Not used to the neighborhood yet. I got here recently, too."

"Not at all! Honestly. We just needed a project."

"Well. I appreciate it."

Another person would have asked questions. As soon as they were gone, he'd think of some.

For now, nothing occurred to him. He was a deer in the headlights.

"You have a lovely home," he ventured.

"Oh! Yes. So do you."

That was established now—they both had lovely homes. They'd bought them with money.

The children turned to go, and he reached out to put the pie down on a ledge. To allow him to shut the door.

Ardis started to follow them, then swiveled and looked back at him. Smiled with a new animation—as if, having performed the small talk, she was released into the real.

"When we decided to get the place—I mean, I fell in love with it, so—but I did worry," she said. "About the glass wall. I thought, wow, whoever lives next door is going to have a human fish tank to look at. There used to be this tinting on it, to make it more one-way? But over the years it faded, I guess. It's this specialty firm that does the re-tinting, and they have a long waiting list. I didn't know how long, at first. And with the screens up, after a while, I start to feel claustrophobic. So I just wanted to say, for now, I hope it's not too annoying. Our fish-tank reality show. Over there."

He struggled to find the right words.

"Yeah, I've—I try not to stare. On purpose. But it's kind of—it's the landscape there *is*. I just look out. And then I feel like a Peeping Tom."

Behind his mother, Tom glanced up. Summoned.

"Oh—sorry. An expression."

He wanted to kick himself. Right off the bat, he was introducing the idea of perverts.

Nice. Coming from the bachelor next door.

"Of course, *anyone* would," Ardis reassured him. Nodded in understanding. "*Anyone* would feel that way."

"Last year, when I bought *this* house, I was back East. I found it online. I'd never visited. I did look at the satellite view. But I didn't really look at the other houses."

"You had no idea you'd have to be a voyeur."

But she smiled again. Sincere.

"Well. I'll try not to be one," he said. He felt sheepish.

"Forget it!" said Ardis. Threw her hands up. "It's not your fault. You should look where you want to. Put your eyes anywhere! When you're inside your own house. You have to be free!"

She had a certain exuberance.

As though anything was possible. And she had nothing to hide.

IN HIS FORMER LIFE, before he left New York, he hadn't noticed birds. He'd thought of them the way you might think of butterflies or flowers—passing impressions of a life elsewhere. He'd pictured tropical kinds. Flurries of color.

But here most of them were brown or gray. The common ones on the castle grounds, anyway. They hopped and pecked. Except for a gray dove that didn't hop. It trundled along with a comical gait—swayed side-to-side, its red feet splayed a bit. Its breast was swelled out. Plump. Front-loaded.

He discovered it was building a nest. Near the top of a sliding door to his back terrace, on a light fixture. Twigs and paper shreds. He took out the bulb, because the light was motion-activated, like all the castle's outdoor lights. He was afraid the nest might catch fire.

Security came to do a sweep. The nest had been there maybe a week, and the gray bird sat on it.

The guy from the company checked the perimeter, the sensors. Replaced a backup battery. Gil followed him around, watching. He saw him spot the nest.

"Should I remove it for you?"

"No!"

"It's just a mourning dove," said the guy. "She'll build one somewhere else in no time flat. We have 'em at my place, too. Make their nests over doorways. And other high-traffic locations. Fly out all bothered and scare the bejaysus out of you. My wife screams. Every time."

"No, but thanks anyway," repeated Gil.

"Without the light, though, your visibility's gonna be compromised."

"That's OK."

THE HUSBAND WASN'T HOME as much as the others. He seemed to work Sundays as well as weekdays, though for shorter hours. He went out after lunch wearing a jacket and tie, returning for dinner.

Their backyards were separated by a fence and two privacy hedges. That way if one neighbor decided to take down a hedge, the other would remain as a barrier. But the castle was two stories atop a slight, sloping hill, and the glass house was one floor, so Gil could see over the hedges.

His yard had desert landscaping, beds of cacti and rocks in the sand. The glass house had a single tall, old tree and a large expanse of grass Tom liked to play on.

He never succeeded in getting his sister to play with him. Through the glass Gil saw him beg before he went outside, but she shook her head and turned back to her phone.

So he went out alone, often wearing padded protective gear: bulky shin guards and arm coverings. Though he had no opponent.

On the lawn he leapt and kicked and chopped the air in a frenzy, shouting *Hi-ya!* And *Hi-yee!*

A martial arts practitioner.

Self-taught, Gil strongly suspected.

Tornado kick! Hi-ya!

After a few days of this, the husband emerged in pajamas one morning and hung a punching bag from their tree. Tom trailed behind him, watched as he tied the bag up. Then landed a series of punishing blows.

The last was a wild, fierce kick. The boy fell awkwardly.

Gil laughed. Not out of meanness but joy.

How long had it been since he laughed out loud? He couldn't recall. At night he watched the political comedy shows, but a smile was all they drew from him.

Tom went limping back to the house with his dad. The limp was theatrically exaggerated.

First he favored one leg, then the other. Just didn't have it down.

SUMMERS WERE SO HOT in the desert that most residents didn't go outside much. This was true of Ardis and her husband, and also of Clem. But it was not true of Tom.

"It's superhuman. Little kids. And temperature. He barely *feels* the heat," said Ardis.

They'd met at the curb, unlocking their mailboxes. Even in this neighborhood, where serious crime was unheard of, most of the boxes had locks.

A matter of principle, evidently.

It wasn't a gated community, but it might as well have been.

"I see him out there by himself a lot," said Gil.

"He hasn't been to school here yet," said Ardis. "So he has no friends."

Gil nodded.

"And he said no to day camp," said Ardis. "Because he has no friends there, either."

"I know the feeling," said Gil.

He had all of two friends, himself. Give or take. Both back East. Vic and Van Alsten.

Married and busy.

Plus Rajiv, who'd been his best friend in college. But when he got engaged, he'd moved to India to be near his wife's family.

The others had slowly fallen away.

"I don't know what to do with Tom," said Ardis. "It's nearly *two more months* till school starts! We limit their screen time. And he reads a lot, but eventually he gets restless."

Her face was fine-boned, its lines both delicate and sleek. She wore big sunglasses, glamorous.

"I need to return your pie plate," he said.

"Did you actually *eat* the pie?" said Ardis. "You can admit it, if you couldn't finish. I won't be offended. Oh! I hope you're not gluten-free? I should have checked. Everyone's gluten-free these days."

"Nah. Old school here, bucking the trend. I welcome gluten. It was very good. Not vegan either. Was there cream cheese in the mix?"

"Sour cream."

"I admit. I ate it in two sittings."

"You should come over!" Enthusiastic, suddenly. Seized by a perfect idea. "Throw a ball with Tom, or something. Would you *mind*? Even ten minutes of your time would be a *godsend*. He's so bored he follows me all around the house. Wherever I go. Like a dog. It's driving me crazy."

He hesitated. What if Tom didn't have any interest in the activity? Complained wearily, Do I *have* to? when she told him. Play ball with some guy I don't even *know*?

He wouldn't blame the kid. Not in the least.

"Believe me," she said quickly. A mind reader. "He's desperate. He'd play ball with a pile of bricks, at this point. No offense. But you wouldn't even have to *talk* to him."

He went back into his house and got the plate, nervous. Was it clean? Was that a stuck-on scrap of crust? He scraped at it with a finger.

No. Just a nick in the glass.

He put on sunglasses of his own. Why had he said he'd go *now*? He could have waited till later.

It was stifling outside. Had to be 110.

But there was something about Ardis. Momentum—you couldn't refuse her. It was easier not to.

Tom answered the door and led him through the living room and dining area.

Gil set the pie plate on the kitchen island. Ardis emerged from somewhere in the core.

"I'm going to take a quick shower," she said. "Clem's reading in her room. Why don't you get some exercise, Tom? Gil said he could throw a ball around with you. Did you put on sunscreen?"

"I hate sunscreen," Tom announced.

"Uh-huh. Did you put it on anyway?"

Tom did a combination nod/headshake.

"Come on!" he said to Gil. "I have a bat. I have a lot of balls. But I don't have a ball machine."

"Well. I mean. *No one* has a ball machine," said Gil.

"This friend of mine does! Donny. In Denver. We lived there before. It's a Lobster Elite Grand Four."

"Oh," said Gil. "Wow. A Lobster."

They went out onto the back deck, down the stairs. Tom threw open a box beside the staircase. Pulled out a plastic bat and a bucket of Wiffle balls.

"I have to play with these," he said. "One time? When we were hitting real softballs? Donny got hit. Ball in the face."

"Ouch," said Gil.

"It wasn't me. It was a kid named Rebel that was fat."

"Ah, fat."

"And really strong. She didn't mean it but. Donny got hit right in the eyeball. An ambulance even came."

"That had to hurt."

"He didn't go blind, though."

"Lucky," said Gil.

"He wore an eye patch. So then his parents got him the Lobster."

"A happy ending."

"Are you a good throw? I'm not a good throw."

"I couldn't say," said Gil. "I'm too modest."

"I like to hit better."

So he pitched and Tom hit. And missed. Many times.

The sun beat down.

"Could I have a glass of water, do you think?" he asked Tom, finally.

He could go back to his house for water, but it might look like he was cutting the ball play short.

"Oh. Water's in the kitchen."

If he went in by himself, maybe Ardis would be emerging from the shower.

An intimacy hazard. Inappropriate.

"Let's go in together. You can show me where it is."

Tom dropped his bat reluctantly.

But in the kitchen he was flummoxed.

"Water comes from the fridge," said Tom, and pointed to the dispenser.

"A glass?"

"I don't know where they *are!*" He looked mildly panicked. "She always *gets* me them!"

Kids these days, Van Alsten would have said, shaking his head.

Van Alsten couldn't stand kids these days. Even his own he could barely tolerate.

Or so he used to claim.

"I'll check here. In the cabinet."

He opened a cabinet door, tentative. Didn't want to overstep. But he was so parched he felt borderline despairing.

"Hey, guys," said Ardis, padding in barefooted. Sure enough: bathrobe. Thick and white, terrycloth. A towel around her hair. Immaculate. No grown person should have such flawless skin.

"Sorry. Was looking for a cup. For water. Thirsty."

"Let me get it," she offered, smiling.

Standing there, drinking, he saw her over the rim of the glass. Still smiling. A sister of mercy.

"I just have a good *feeling* about you," she told him, when he had drained the glass.

The nicest thing a woman had said to him in years.

He had to meet the husband, he decided.

Had no designs on Ardis. But still.

THAT VERY EVENING the husband came to Gil's door. Gil pictured him thinking: This guy's been in my house. I better check him out.

Up close he looked like the debonair spy character on an animated TV show for adults Gil couldn't remember the name of. That sweep of black hair over the forehead.

But the spy character, though cartoonishly handsome, was an abrasive jerk. While the husband was not.

"I could ask to borrow a tool," he said, before an introduction.

"You could," said Gil. "But I don't have many."

"Wouldn't know what to do with it anyway. Circular saw, that's a thing. Right?"

"I believe it is."

"Miter saw? Belt sander?"

"Those are things too."

"Yeah but. I wouldn't know a belt sander if it walked in asking for bourbon. Just wanted to break the ice. I heard you're new in town too."

"I am. Name's Gil."

"I'm Ted. Don't hold it against me. My parents' fault. They were immigrants. From Iran—Persian. Trying to fit in. It's not even Theodore, then Ted for short. Just, literally, Ted. Right on the birth certificate. Maybe they figured if they named me that I'd grow up to play tennis. Wear tennis whites. That's what an American guy named Ted should do."

"Ted's a country-club name. For sure."

"I never picked up tennis, though. Or golf. Clearly a disappointment."

They shook hands.

He invited Ted in. It was the mention of bourbon. His favorite place in the house was the bar. J-shaped against one wall, built in the days when living-room bars were A-OK. Status symbols. Rather than signals of alcoholism.

It had wood paneling and glass doors, and the wood paneling was a single panel, gradually curving.

"Nice," said Ted. He sat on a barstool. It had a revolving seat, so he revolved.

Gil liked how he spun around on the barstool. Un-self-conscious. The way a kid would.

He stepped behind the counter. Bartending covered his social anxiety.

He'd once had a job doing it, at a gay bar in Chelsea soon after he moved from Boston to New York, and actually he'd loved the work. But eventually he'd quit, out of guilt. Watching people drop off their résumés, then get turned down. Some other guy *needed* the income.

It was a problem he'd had with all jobs, since he discovered he was rich. Someone else needed them.

Tending bar was the only paying gig he'd ever had.

Ted talked about his own work, which had to do with the funding of infrastructure projects. In other countries, Asia primarily. They'd moved here for his recent promotion. Ardis could do her job anywhere, though the decision had been difficult. She hadn't wanted to leave her clients behind. But she was talented, and there was ample demand. Most of the old clients had opted to stay with her, anyway. Do video or phone sessions.

She was a psychotherapist, he said.

She hadn't mentioned it to Gil yet, but it made sense. She was a natural at conversation. Confident in her instincts.

Maybe she was being so friendly as an extension of her career—recognized in him a person who'd never had therapy, but sorely needed it.

Then again, maybe she got that all the time. Maybe a therapist was suspected of being professional in every act of personal kindness.

For a guy with movie-star looks, Ted was surprisingly humble. And easygoing. Didn't need to monopolize.

The older Gil got, the more he noticed people talking about themselves. To the exclusion of everything else. It was the norm of talking. As though the self was the only officially sanctioned topic.

Ted didn't do that. He tried to draw Gil out a bit but wasn't insistent. The only things Gil said about himself were, I don't work for a living. Used to volunteer, when I lived back East. More or less full time. But not here. Yet.

And one remark on the subject of marriage. No, I never married, he said, when Ted asked if he was divorced.

Forgive the question, but all his friends were divorced, Ted said. You practically felt like a pariah, as a non-divorced person.

I was with someone for a long time, but we never got married, Gil told him.

Ted tactfully changed the subject.

They had two drinks each, and Ted genially left.

BY THE TIME the mourning dove's two chicks flew out of the nest, they looked just like her—only a fraction smaller. He could barely tell the babies from the mother.

AS THE SUMMER wore on he became Tom's shadow—half babysitter, half friend. Ardis was sometimes in the background, but not always. She had a few sessions by phone or at her new office. More as the weeks passed. She was picking up clients.

She seemed to believe he was good company for Tom. A bachelor, yes. But not a threat.

Her trust pleased him. Ardis was all invitation—openness.

He wondered about it. Then thought he'd settled on an explanation: she was like someone who'd never been hurt.

There was pitching and hitting, and there was holding black pads so Tom could punch and kick them. Gil tried to mix it up, brought out an old croquet set and badminton racquets. Tom scrunched up his face at the sight of these antiques, but then was persuaded.

When the heat got too much for Gil he moved them inside, and they switched to board games.

Clem tended to retreat to her bedroom when they went in. She was four years older than her brother—nearly fifteen, she said—

and missed the friends she'd had to leave behind. She spent a lot of time group-messaging them, looking at their selfies with cat- and dog-ear filters, glued to her phone. She was polite to Gil but impersonal.

Clem was short for Clementine, she told him, but it sounded too much like the fruit.

A couple of times she joined them for a board game, which she played well but didn't seem to enjoy much. Tom adored her but got on her nerves.

Gil had the feeling she gave him a small measure of credit for creating a distraction.

ON THE SATELLITE RADIO in his car there was a medical channel he tuned in to sometimes. Doctor Radio, out of NYU Langone. The hosts of one show, a psychology call-in deal, discussed "complicated" grief.

"Persistent" grief, another term.

It wasn't him, he thought. Was it?

Death was the form of loss the show was focused on.

Some of the bereaved still stared at photos for hours every day, a full three or four years after their loved one had died. One father brought up his dead child's name or tastes in even the most casual conversation. Or no conversation at all.

"He liked the kind of cheese that comes in single slices," the father would muse, if a cheese platter was passed to him at a get-together. "American. Processed. That was the only cheese he'd ever eat. I used to think, you know, that he'd grow out of it. One day."

When someone asked if the father wanted a window open, he would say, "He always wanted to be near an open window. Beside his bed, when he was sick, there was a window that faced north. He wanted the blinds up. No matter what. He wanted to watch the world go by."

Gil did not do any of these things. His loss was of a lower order.

But he did have a question. It was a question no one could answer except her.

And she'd never answered it.

QUAIL

AT THE BACK of his garden the fence had holes. The property abutted a dry, sandy riverbed on public land. One of the reasons he'd bought it: suburban, but next to rolling foothills studded with prickly green vegetation. Dramatic formations of sandstone that cropped up out of nowhere.

They called the dry rivers washes, here in Arizona. In New Mexico, arroyos.

Bushes grew in the braiding strands of the wash. Cacti called prickly pears and cholla. Straggling trees with gray bark that bloomed in clouds of pale violet.

He had it on his to-do list to get the fence fixed, until he realized wildlife came through the holes to drink from his small artificial pond. Among them were families of birds with black plumes on their heads.

These birds were round-bodied and high-strung, flushing out in a flurry of wingbeats when he approached. Or running away quickly, in an ungainly fashion. Their plumes hung over their faces, between their eyes, and trembled as they ran.

It was as though they were unwitting recipients of the face feathers—the plumes had landed on the fronts of their heads. And stuck.

Gave them the look of foolish dandies.

ARDIS HAD PLANNED a week-long vacation for the family in July. They were flying to a resort near Aspen, where it was cool and there were mountain breezes.

Tom said he didn't *want* to go. Aspen was dumb. He'd already been there. A bunch of times. They made him go to stores. Mostly so Clem could buy more boring clothes. She always wanted clothes. The only thing she wanted more than clothes was makeup. And lotions.

Guess what, he said to Gil. In the bathroom she had *eleven* lip glosses. She had eight things of mascara. He wasn't allowed to touch them. But he'd counted them with his eyes.

Some of their friends had a house in Aspen, which Ardis referred to as a cabin. Though Gil had difficulty picturing it as small, square, and made of logs.

The friends' son was about Tom's age. Waterslides were promised. And lazy rivers.

Gil agreed to take care of the indoor plants for them. Ted said they could have used a service but hadn't had time to select one.

Anyway, Ardis said, she felt better having Gil watch over the place.

She walked him through the house telling him how much water the different plants needed. He wrote it down on a penciled floor plan he was making.

Small circles for the plants.

"You're so organized," said Ardis, admiring.

Ted warned him the security system had cameras. When they went away, they'd turn on the ones inside. "So don't, like, pick your nose," he said. "We might see it."

"I never pick my nose," said Gil.

"Never?" said Ted. "A bold statement."

"I like to think it's accurate," said Gil.

WITH THE FAMILY AWAY he barely knew how to spend his days. It had always been hard, finding the best way to contribute.

One of his many efforts was how he'd met Vic and Van Alsten, more than a decade ago. He'd signed up to volunteer at a center for refugee families, figuring a language barrier might help him avoid the delicacies of interaction. Make things more basic, less subtle.

They were short-staffed, so he had his pick of tasks. He'd put in forty hours a week doing clerical work, paying the bills and maximizing efficiency, converting the center's filing system from paper to electronic. Taught himself new programs to do it.

Vic came in a couple of nights a week to teach English to the refugees. His focus was those from the Americas, since Spanish was his first language. He and Gil went out for a beer some evenings when he finished his class, before he took the train back to his family's apartment in Hoboken.

Vic was a kindly man, a public-school teacher and devout Catholic.

Enter Van Alsten, whose wife had issued an ultimatum. Stop drinking so much, she said, and do something productive. Or there would have to be changes.

She hadn't said what the changes would be, but they didn't sound good.

He didn't like his given name, he told Gil. It had never suited him. In fact he had a strict nondisclosure policy on the subject. He went by his last, ever since prep school.

There were family funds. From his wife's side, mostly. He managed their stock holdings hunched over a computer till the markets closed.

But his wife didn't approve of how he spent his free time lately: liquor. And TV.

He'd played basketball at Yale, so he figured he might as well play it with refugees. Be a kind of athletic mentor, he said. There was a gym at the center and kids with time on their hands.

He didn't *get* kids, he told Gil in the office when he appeared the first night to start his coaching gig.

He gazed into the middle distance, head cocked.

A kid took up space, he said, but—in the short term, anyway—seemed to fulfill no useful function. Back in the days of family farms, you could put them to work in the fields once they were big enough to dig up the dirt. Now they just hung around, eating, sleeping, gathering numerous objects, and waiting to become fully formed. A kid was like an ornamental vase placed awkwardly at the edge of a doorway. You stubbed your toe on the damn thing every time you passed.

But actually, worse than a vase. Because a vase didn't run around emitting senseless noise and asking for handouts.

Still, his distaste for children wouldn't stop him. He was going to mentor the shit out of them.

And why, you might ask?

Gil hadn't asked, but Van Alsten told him anyway. He explained quite clearly. It was the ultimatum. He didn't want to lose his wife. She was his best friend, hands down, but also, she had the best ass he had ever seen.

He felt bad for other heterosexual men, that the ass of his wife was off-limits to them. He wanted to take it out on parade, so others could get the benefit, he said. Purely in a visual sense, of course. And if he was honest, he felt bad on his own account as well. A man has his vanity. We all do, he said. We don't like to admit it, but we do.

Since no one else could see the ass, they couldn't know its beauty. They'd give him more respect. If they fully understood what he was dealing with.

For his wife dressed modestly. And was very stubborn about it. He'd tried to move her toward tight jeans, which in his view were the only acceptable jeans, he said, in terms of women's fashion. He didn't hold with so-called mom jeans. Or the wide-legged hippie ones. Skinny jeans only, please and thank you. He'd given her several gifts of these, as well as leather pants and—on one occasion that ended, unfortunately, in a couples' argument—latex.

His wife never touched the gifts. Unwrapping them, she

smiled patiently and shook her head. Later they showed up in boxes headed for Goodwill.

She stuck to skirts that didn't cling, and, when pruning the roses on the terrace of their apartment, a pair of baggy canvas overalls. With daubs of paint on them.

And for shoes, a pair of ratty high-tops left over from her teenage years.

That was what you got, he said, for marrying old money.

His plan was, treat the refugee kids the same way he treated everyone else. Which Gil guessed was, rudely.

Gil walked him back to the gymnasium and introduced him to the teens, who were playing a disorganized and not-so-technical game. Hung out a few minutes and watched Van Alsten take charge.

He was a surprisingly good player. Even excellent. The kids were impressed.

But he also had a tic. If you could call it that.

He narrated everything he did in a string of vile curses. Curse words emerged from his mouth in an unending stream as he ran, dribbled, jumped, and shot. The worst ones you could think of were the ones that came out of him.

The kids gaped, as Gil did. But then he noticed them begin to smile. Some laughed behind their hands, shyly.

They were full-on enjoying it.

The next night Van Alsten invited him out for a drink. Since the usual beer was already planned with Vic, they all went over together. An Irish bar across the street.

Van Alsten's crude talk put Vic off at first. Then he seemed to decide, like the kids, that the patter was a running joke. Van Alsten didn't need to be taken at his word—he was a performance. Somehow likable, both despite and because of it. He was often funny, and it let him get away with things.

After that it was always the three of them. They couldn't have shaken Van Alsten if they wanted to.

But they didn't.

He drank two double vodka tonics for their one beer. Then bragged about his temperance.

He was a big man, though, and seemed to hold his liquor well. The only sign he'd had too much was that he began to allude to his time in the Navy. The best-run outfit in the armed forces, he claimed.

He'd been an officer, apparently—a tradition in his family. Served in Afghanistan. Leading a reconstruction team, as they called it.

He'd tell a brief story about someone he'd known there. Served with. Or sometimes a local. Then he'd trail off, eyes watering.

Vic would put a hand on his back, say it was probably time to head out. School day tomorrow, after all, said Vic.

The three of them stayed friends when the refugee center shut down—Gil's campaign to maximize efficiency hadn't quite done the trick.

In the years that followed, he tended to see the two men separately. Possibly Vic preferred Van Alsten in smaller doses. Instead of joining them for drinks, he'd claim a family obligation, then invite Gil over on his own. Gil met his wife and children, attended Saturday barbecues in Jersey and once a daughter's confirmation.

Meanwhile Van Alsten found a new basketball game, telling his wife he was still volunteering. With an "underserved community."

The game was actually with some older kids, as well as a number of grown men, who played up in Harlem. And weren't exactly looking to be mentored.

Gil sometimes met up with him as these games were ending, watching from the other side of a chain-link fence.

He seemed truly happy when he played.

Plus the older kids were almost as foulmouthed as him.

THE PLUMED BIRDS were quail. Ground-nesters, supposedly, but now and then they got flustered and made poor choices of nest locations. He found a desert-bird website run by enthusiastic ornithologists. Read accounts of the quail building their nests high up on balconies, where their clutches of ten to twelve eggs would hatch and then the chicks, evolved to be late fliers, plummeted to their deaths.

Luckily their nesting season was over.

HE NEEDED TO GET TO WORK again—idleness was depressing.

One of the groups he supported had a mission of helping homeless gay youth. There was a big-brother program. But on the phone with the volunteer coordinator, he got the distinct impression that, in terms of working directly with the youth, his non-gayness took him out of the running.

How the guy knew he wasn't gay was anyone's guess. A major-donor database, possibly.

The coordinator's dismissal offended him a bit. He told Van Alsten about it on the phone.

Van Alsten said he would have retorted, Oh yeah? You want me to be gay? I'll be as gay as fuck, you little shit.

Van Alsten made him laugh. But he wasn't Van Alsten.

And once the defensiveness receded, he had to accept it made sense.

He called a conservation group next, to which his sexual preference could be of no possible interest. Oh, yes! He could come in and help fold leaflets, the coordinator said.

Weren't there machines that did that now? he asked. She chuckled and didn't answer.

Gil said thanks, he'd think about it. He wasn't sure leaflet-folding was the best use of his particular skill set.

Third he called up an abused women's shelter he'd also started funding. He hesitated, knowing it could easily go south, an offer to help out there.

But he'd learned from the annual report that the shelter, following in the footsteps of a sister group in California, allowed the presence of male volunteers. A pilot program. Its management believed the guests needed a few men they could trust.

The application process could take some time, the woman on the phone told him, because they were *extremely* selective. Being well intentioned isn't enough, she explained. We need men with a reassuring manner.

References, a criminal background check. There will be interviews, if your initial screening tests check out.

Thank you, he said.

Alone in the castle, he practiced walking around slowly, making no sudden movements.

ASPEN HAD BEEN A BLAST, Tom said. He came back with a farmer's tan. He'd been outside a lot. The kid he'd spent time with was an *awesome* snowboarder. Not in the summer, obviously. But he'd seen videos. The kid, Javier, had his own YouTube channel.

Javier was his current idol. And had taught him to skateboard. His summer pursuit.

Ardis had been reluctant to allow it. She knew of a boy who'd lost his spleen in a skateboarding accident.

"A *spleen*," said Tom contemptuously. "What *is* a spleen? What does a spleen even *do*?"

Gil admitted he didn't have all the facts on spleens.

Once Tom was suited up in knee pads, wrist guards, and a top-notch helmet, Ardis had given her consent.

He skated on their two driveways and out in the cul-de-sac while Gil supervised, keeping a lookout for cars.

Holding a silver umbrella to keep off the sun.

THE SCREENING TESTS were passed. Letters of recommendation from previous volunteer posts and an affidavit from Gil's lawyer. It said he'd never been convicted of a felony or misdemeanor.

When he went in to be interviewed, he wore a collared shirt with a sweater on top. It made him look like someone's dorky uncle. Gave himself a close shave, in case his usual five o'clock shadow lent him an overly manly aspect.

He had to be buzzed in at a staff entrance on the side. They didn't want strange men filing in through the women's living quarters.

The director he met with reminded him of a nun he'd met at a Christmas party of Vic's. But she wasn't a nun, just a regular lesbian. Happily married. There were several pictures of her and her wife on the desk. Lest any doubt remained, she spoke in glowing terms of their three corgis.

Whom she referred to as "the kiddos."

The interview seemed to go well enough, though he felt she asked a lot of questions related to his view of violent offenders. As though there might be a wide range of reasonable but differing opinions.

"I do see one stumbling block," she told him, as the conversation wound down.

"Stumbling block?"

"Your looks. They're a potential disadvantage."

"My looks," he repeated, mumbling.

"You're fairly attractive." Her tone was punitive.

"Oh?" he said, startled. "I never . . ."

"I'm not saying it's a deal-breaker," she told him. "But it could be seen as threatening."

"I mean, I think . . . sort of average?"

He felt flattered, but skeptical. Considered adding: if she thought *he* was threatening, she should get a load of the guy who lived next door to him.

"We tend to select men that are physically more like Jason

over there," she said, and inclined her head sideways, toward an interior office window.

Beyond it stood a short, potbellied guy with a potato-shaped head, crushed-in face, and wispy comb-over. He was scrutinizing his fingernails.

"Ah, oh," said Gil. "I didn't know that was a condition."

"As I say, just a heads-up. We'll see what happens at the interview with the board. They're very hands-on."

HE MADE DINNER at the glass house with Tom helping. He'd mentioned to Ardis that he enjoyed cooking but, living alone, had gotten rusty.

"Pasta?" she'd said. "They always want it, and I'm so tired of making mac and cheese and spaghetti with sauce from a jar. What do you think? You and Tom could do it together. This afternoon. I have a phone session. And it's supposed to rain."

The monsoon storms had arrived. Not what they used to be, the locals claimed.

In the olden days, several weeks or months of rain had poured down in torrents. The wash behind the street had run with several feet of water that swept along it in a brown froth, churning up leaf litter and debris.

Now they were lucky if the wash ran hard once in a season. Climate change, some said.

But the sky was dark with banks of clouds, and there was moisture in the air. A warm wind whipped the trees around. Lightning and thunder were predicted.

Cooking dinner might be an opportunity, he thought, to

familiarize Tom with the location of drinking cups in his own home. Even some bowls and plates.

He swung by the market and picked up ingredients.

Tom wasn't "super excited" to help make dinner, he told Gil candidly.

"Just run with it," said Gil. "As a favor to your mother. Hey: she told me she wants you to audition for one of those competitive kid-chef shows. You know. Where you cook in a contest? On TV?"

"No way!" said Tom, staring at him.

Hard to say whether he believed it for a second or it was sheer pretense.

They made pasta from scratch using a machine Gil had brought over. Tom got into it. Clem wandered through the kitchen at one point, bored, so he had her scrub in and let her help too.

Tom retained a few minutes' seniority and tried to boss her around a bit.

"Shut up, you don't know anything," Clem told him.

Hmm. Spirited.

"I'm telling you said shut up."

"Go ahead."

"It's a swear word."

"Don't be dumb. They only called it a swear word in *kindergarten.*"

"I'm telling you said I was dumb, then."

"Tattling is beneath your dignity, Tom," said Gil. "Far beneath it."

"I don't know what that means," said Tom.

He had egg on his face. A smear of yolk on one cheek.

"You're a skateboarder," said Gil. "You're way too cool for telling on people."

"Ha," said Clem. "As *if*."

"Skateboarding's not a crime," said Tom.

"That's, like, a *bumper sticker*, Tom. You're *so* annoying!" said Clem.

Tom took the insult in stride.

He was used to them, it appeared.

Still, by the time Ardis and Ted got home they'd laid on a fine spread. Clem cut some wildflowers from Gil's yard and made them into a centerpiece. Rain spattered onto the glass walls. In the distance thunder rolled.

"We have two sauces," he told the assembled company once they were seated. "One involves butter and grated parmesan. The other is a melon sauce. Cream, cantaloupe, pancetta, and marjoram."

"It's weird," said Tom.

"Yes. The weird sauce is for the daring among you. I'm not judging. Except to say, fortune favors the brave."

"I'll have that one," said Ted. "Hands down."

"Me too," said Ardis.

"I'll have the parmesan, please," said Clem.

"I'll try one bite," said Tom.

Tom thought of himself as a vegetarian, said Ardis.

He hadn't mentioned this previously.

However, he *did* make an exception for salami, she amended. And pepperoni, also.

Tom ate a large plateful.

Afterward the children watched a movie and Gil sat with Ardis and Ted, drinking wine and gazing out at the rain and forks of lightning on the horizon.

Gil talked about his failing attempts to participate in society.

Ted talked about a guy at the office who wouldn't take hints on the subject of body odor and was, unbeknownst to him, running a serious risk of being fired for it. None of the managers could bring themselves to tackle the problem head-on.

On paper, of course, that wouldn't be the reason.

"*You* should do it, Ted," said Ardis. "Take him aside. It'd be a humanitarian mission."

"See, now, I was afraid you'd say that."

Ardis said she couldn't discuss her clients, although she'd relish telling them about the gentleman who had a fetish for seasonal lawn ornaments. Not naming any names, but the lawn ornaments included Santa Claus. And his eight reindeer. A coy squirrel with paws held up to mouth, expressing: Speak No Evil.

And one garden gnome, bent over smiling with his pants down. There was a bluebird perched on his bare, ceramic ass.

"Get out," said Ted. "There's no such lawn ornament in existence."

"Oh, but there is," said Ardis.

She told Gil how she and Ted first met.

It was their junior year, and Ted had just taken a bad fall off a cliff during a hike. He had a scar on his forehead—he raised his sweep of black hair to show it—and at the time he'd considered the incident to have been a close brush with death. As a result he was very dramatic during that period, thinking deep thoughts about mortality.

He'd read French novels. Poems about solitude.

"I was the hero of my own story," he said. "It was one man against the wild. To have survived, I must have had a destiny."

"He decided his destiny was me," said Ardis.

"I would not leave her alone," said Ted.

"It wasn't a slam dunk, at first," agreed Ardis. "I was dating other people."

"She was the bigger catch."

"He's aged well," said Ardis.

"At the time, gangly."

"Plus acne along the hairline," added Ardis.

"You hit below the belt," said Gil.

"I wish she was lying," said Ted.

"We had a class together," said Ardis. "Abnormal Psych."

"I was just auditing," said Ted. "Because I saw her walking across the quad and followed her in."

"Stalking," said Gil, "they call it now."

"Nineteen-year-old males are pretty much the dregs," said Ted.

"You were cute," said Ardis. "Once I got past the pimples."

"Persistence," said Ted, pouring more wine for each of them. "A cliché, but. The most useful trait there is. In business and in love."

Gil wasn't sure about that. It hadn't worked for him.

HE'D MET LANE at a pool hall on Houston Street. He was there with his money manager's assistant and a group of his friends. Recent college graduates like him.

The assistant wouldn't last long at the job, in the end—he'd been hired because of a family connection.

He was a pleasant guy, if a bit low energy. *Work ethic* wasn't a phrase that resonated with him.

Too Protestant, man, he said.

He got stoned a lot and told meandering tales. Mostly

about the hijinks he'd gotten into wandering through derelict buildings and being chased off by security guards. Or cops. He never stole anything, but he liked abandoned places.

This was soon after the trust was distributed, when Gil was still learning how not to seem disgustingly rich. Without lying.

He'd always been bad at lying. Never needed to, as a child. His grandmother had been strict, even severe, but hands-off. As long as he read a lot, she'd left him to his own devices. And it hadn't occurred to him to disobey her.

After she died, he didn't have many people to practice lying on. Then he discovered he didn't like to do it.

If Gil refused to lie, the money manager had said—though he put it differently: *dissembling*—he would have to learn when to be suspicious of people's motives. And when not to.

But suspicion didn't come easily to Gil either.

Since he didn't know anyone else in the city—he'd moved there mainly to get away from Boston—he went out with the junior staff for a while. They were friendly and available. They went to movies, clubs and bars. And sometimes billiards or bowling.

One night Gil was playing pool with them when the stoner assistant's girlfriend arrived with another woman. They stood by a counter along the wall, watching and sipping beer as the game ended.

After a while the stoner's girlfriend, who was also a stoner, came up to him and whispered in his ear: My friend thinks you're cute. Her name is Lane.

THE SHELTER'S BOARD of directors was all women. Some were in business attire, taking a break from their corporate workdays, harried and checking their phones as the interview began. Others seemed dressed for leisure, earth tones and flowing garments.

The kind worn by Van Alsten's wife, possibly.

He'd never met her—there'd been two or three near misses, but somehow their two couples hadn't ended up getting together—so she was an indistinct figure. Forever pruning her roses in beat-up Converse on the terrace of a penthouse.

Inside the director's office they sat in a ring on folding chairs. Gil introduced himself and took a vacant seat.

"As you know, we're looking for male escorts," said one of the board members.

Gil held back a nervous grin with some effort. No other person present seemed to hear the double meaning.

"Some of our guests—when they start to go out again, maybe shopping or just to the post office or their kids' schools—feel safer with a man beside them," she went on. "Occasionally there's a run-in with an abuser."

"It doesn't happen a lot," said another, "but we *have* had incidents. There's a protocol we'd teach you, and you'd call the police immediately—often there's a restraining order in place—but would you feel comfortable in that role?"

"I would," said Gil.

WHEN HE'D TOLD VIC and Van Alsten about the walk he was planning, they thought he was certifiable. In Vic's case, maybe even selfish. Or at least self-indulgent.

Though he put it more diplomatically.

Van Alsten said Gil was full of shit. He'd give it up inside a week.

He listened to them and didn't argue. They might both be right.

And then he left.

He'd sent postcards of scenic vistas to Vic, and to Van Alsten he'd texted an occasional picture.

From West Virginia, a decrepit gas station with the peeling remnants of a pin-up girl pasted on its brick wall.

From Alabama, a photo he'd taken inside a diner, where every last patron was smoking except a baby in a highchair.

NEAR THE BEGINNING of the long walk, while he was mostly away from the news cycle and the screens, something in the country had rumbled and shifted. He'd woken up one morning in a dingy motel and turned on the TV as he dressed.

To find it was the day after the election.

He hadn't registered the date, the night before—he consulted his phone calendar sporadically, mostly to check on his progress— but now it was November 9th.

He'd mailed in his ballot before he left, his final civic act as a New Yorker, and assumed politics would proceed as they usually did. Though likely, this time, there'd be a woman managing the compromises and the mediocrities. That, at least, might be of some interest.

But the new president wasn't a reasonable, compromising woman—quite the opposite.

He'd called Van Alsten, then Vic. They too were stunned. Van Alsten said, Our problem is we still have fucking hope. That's our problem.

I just don't understand, said Vic. I just don't understand.

He'd walked in the shock of it for days. Even weeks. Around him, signs and billboards he'd scoffed at before loomed like warnings after the fact.

He looked out at the fields and woods as he passed, at the train tracks and industrial parks and outlet malls. And thought of a B movie he'd once watched with Lane where giant worms burrowed, invisible, beneath the soil.

Then suddenly erupted out of the ground and opened their gaping maws. Lined with impossible teeth.

THE WALK was when he first noticed birds. Vultures, hawks, and once what he believed to be an eagle. Like him, they were mostly alone.

He wondered about their lives. Their solitude, broken only by courtship and breeding.

Overhead he sometimes glimpsed flocks of smaller birds. In their far-off, swooping dances the flocks imparted to him a vague longing.

Birds were descendants of the dinosaurs, they'd taught him in college. This was different from what they'd taught him when he was in elementary school.

Paleontology was progressing by leaps and bounds, they said. It was no longer held to be true that all the dinosaurs had gone extinct sixty-six million years ago, after the Chicxulub impactor made its crater in Mexico. Blocked out the sun. And killed off the plants the dinosaurs needed to survive.

Only the ones that wouldn't turn into birds.

There were about three thousand active satellites up in the sky, he'd read. Some twenty-thousand pieces of orbital debris. At any given moment, an average of nine thousand passenger planes flying.

And yet, he'd thought as he walked, without the last of the dinosaurs the sky would be empty.

HUMMINGBIRDS

ARDIS BROUGHT HIM a hummingbird feeder and hung it in a tree whose branches stretched over the back terrace. She came over every few days to replace the sugar water.

She liked changing it out, she said, and didn't want her gift to be a chore for him. The nectar could spoil in the summer sun and then make the hummingbirds sick.

He never found out what species they were—didn't have much interest in classifying them. They were hovering jewels, some shimmering turquoise and purple, others a coppery orange.

They were also highly territorial, and for the sake of nectar he saw one stab another.

Hard. With its needle-like beak.

THE FIRST GUEST he escorted was named Lori and suffered, like many of the people who took refuge at the shelter, from post-traumatic stress.

She wanted to go to the dollar store to buy toys for her little girl. When they fled their apartment, she hadn't had time to bring many. The ones they offered in the communal playroom no longer held her daughter's interest.

He was an unpaid bodyguard, though he lacked both the bulk and the expertise. A bodyguard was all he had permission to be. Not a confidant or advisor, benefactor or friend. They'd been clear on that point during training.

Still, it pained him to see her spend what little cash she had on vinyl trinkets that off-gassed chemicals and made your fingers smell.

But the worst thing someone like him could do, the volunteer coordinator had said, was try to "act like a white knight."

A white knight might believe he was helping a guest by splurging on her, driving to some upscale mall and showering her children with costly gifts. The likes of which they'd never seen before.

And would not see again.

In the long run, the coordinator had said firmly, a white knight would only hurt the guests.

Resist the urge, she instructed.

As he walked up and down the aisles he scouted around for the abusive husband, a veteran of the war in Iraq. The coordinator had AirDropped a photo: bearded, with thick eyebrows and a weather-beaten face.

A bear of a man. Also with post-traumatic stress.

It was contagious.

No bearlike man appeared, and items were found and purchased. One was a rubbery Barbie knockoff that came with a build-it-yourself plastic bed, made of spaghetti-thin, pink tubes you stuck together. Lori said her girl wouldn't care much for the doll but would like to build the bed.

The second was a large water shooter. It resembled a military-grade rifle. "She's a tomboy," said Lori. "And plus, you know, her daddy was a soldier."

Third was a lumpy stuffed creature. Whether it was meant to evoke a mammal, reptile, or fish was unclear. It was purple and plush, with a limbless body that might equally have been a fish or a seal. Sad, round black eyes.

It *represented* animals, Gil thought. Maybe that was enough. A lumpy ambassador.

Lori sat in the passenger seat with the toys spread out on her lap as he drove them back to the shelter.

"You think she'll like them?" she asked.

"Of course she will," said Gil dutifully.

And she did.

VAN ALSTEN TEXTED at 2 a.m. Eastern time. Said he was coming through the Phoenix airport in a couple of weeks, flying to Napa with his wife for some pretentious wine-tasting bullshit. They had a five-hour layover. Would Gil join them for dinner?

Gil texted back yes.

He was glad he'd get to see Van Alsten again.

IN THE LETDOWN that followed his Colorado trip, Tom agreed to attend a one-week camp in kids' martial arts. His father had discovered it, a daily class at a dojo in Tempe.

"Usually it's Ardis who books things, but I had to take the initiative," Ted told Gil.

Ardis's mind was closed to martial arts. It wasn't that she actively objected, more that she simply didn't seem to hear Tom when he talked about it. He followed her around describing the grappling and sparring he wished to do.

He talked about jujitsu, kickboxing, catch wrestling, and karate.

But to Ardis it was as if he wasn't speaking.

This also happened with conversations that Ted himself instigated on the subject of football or soccer. When he brought up a game or player or statistic to Ardis, he told Gil, he had the sensation that his face had turned transparent. She gazed right through it to the future, another time and place without this jangling cascade of arbitrary noise.

Gil could relate. He could throw a ball around and run, but he'd never been a fan of spectator sports. To him they seemed like the Roman Forum—arenas for performing male aggression.

He wasn't aggressive enough for them.

"Was she ever into it?" he asked. "Listening to you talk about sports?"

When he'd started seeing Lane she'd seemed deeply attentive as he talked about various opinions and ideas he had. She'd met his eyes, leaned forward, and nodded intently. As though quite fascinated.

Over time she'd ceased to appear so fascinated.

"I *doubt* it," said Ted. "It just, like, took me years to realize the look on her face wasn't adoration."

"When you're a young guy, it's easy to mistake a woman's boredom for rapture."

ONE DAY HE PICKED TOM up at the dojo when Ardis and Ted both had to work late unexpectedly. He showed up early and watched from behind a viewing window.

The students grappled in pairs while the instructor walked around the room, making corrections. Tom was pinned beneath a much larger boy for several minutes. He looked younger than usual in his loose-fitting white outfit, thin wrists sticking out of the wide sleeves.

Finally the big boy stopped sitting on him.

The teacher gathered the students into rows and spoke a proverb, or maybe a motivational saying.

"In martial arts," he announced, "we do not weed out the weak. We *train* the weak. To be the strong!"

Walking out to the parking lot, Tom had acquired his dramatic limp again.

"You hurt your leg?" asked Gil.

"That big kid kind of crunched it," said Tom.

"He *was* big."

"He's big, but he's not good."

"Oh no?"

Tom shrugged. "Before you got there I was in a pretty dominant position."

"Ah."

"I'm really good at shrimping."

By the time they reached Gil's car the limp had already vanished. Tom chattered on about shrimping, which involved squirming and twisting on the floor.

MARI WANTED to go to a Sunday service at her church, where the uncle who had abused her was also a member of the congregation.

She had a nervous, frail affect—Gil wondered if she'd always been that way or if her fearfulness had been taught to her by the uncle. She was anxious as they went in. Kept her head down. Her hands shook as they walked down the aisle, and she clutched at his arm briefly. Gil consulted his phone, checking the mug shot.

Although it wasn't a mug shot. It was a zoomed-in detail from a group photo, where the uncle was grinning and looking as cheerful as everyone else.

He had a pockmarked face and a low brown ponytail.

They sat down in the pew. When was the last time he'd set foot in a house of worship?

Vic's daughter's confirmation.

Mari looked toward the altar. Nothing would distract her. The spread-out crowd was a body, and she was part of it. On the hymnal her hands stopped shaking.

During Vic's daughter's confirmation the priest had said, "The peace of the Lord be with you always." Then he'd explained: "The words I've just spoken are not *my* words. They are the words of the risen Christ."

Though not a believer, Gil had been hypnotized. He'd had a

strong impression of words emblazoned on the air, soaring upward as the worshippers stood in place. Down through the centuries. Ancient pillars of faith.

"We proclaim your death, O Lord," murmured the congregation now. "Until you come again."

Gil scanned the many rows of heads constantly, on the lookout for low ponytails.

"The Lord be with you," said the priest.

"And with your spirit," said everyone else.

HUMMINGBIRDS ARE THE SMALLEST of birds, he read on the ornithology website. But they have the largest brains, relative to the rest of their bodies.

In those grain-of-rice-sized brains, one scientist wrote, they have exceptional memories. They may even retain an impression of every flowering plant they've ever visited.

How could the birds remember all that? And what research had produced such information?

There was a map of one hummingbird's migration, from Alaska to Mexico.

All by themselves, as summer drew to a close, the tiny birds could fly four thousand miles.

HE MET VAN ALSTEN and his wife at Sky Harbor, in a Mexican-themed restaurant outside security. On the wall hung brightly colored, sequined sombreros. It was lit with tube lights and had a generic grease-and-Lysol sheen.

They stood up promptly when he entered. Van Alsten made the introductions. "My friend Gil. Gil, my wife Constance," he said, formal.

"Call me Connie."

Despite Van Alsten's description, Connie wasn't wearing sack-shaped clothing. She had on a well-cut trench coat and beneath it a pale, cream-colored sweater that looked like cashmere.

Freckles across a sweet, amiable face.

As Gil sat down Van Alsten said, raising his hands palm-up, "Hope you appreciate the place we chose. The food's just OK, but man, the atmosphere!"

It had been over fifteen minutes—they'd ordered drinks and a red-plastic basket of tortilla chips had arrived—when Gil realized that Van Alsten hadn't sworn once.

Not even a gosh darn.

He talked about the irritations of air travel as Connie inclined her head, attentive.

"My brother never flies commercial," said Van Alsten. "You know, the one who's a VC? And has his own jet? Well. He's a part owner. One of those time-share jet deals."

"Disturbing," offered Connie. She was soft-spoken. "The carbon footprint. Painful to contemplate."

"Connie doesn't let us fly private," said Van Alsten. "It came up—when was it? Thanksgiving. At one of my brother's vacation homes. In Nantucket. The white Caribbean, he calls it. No irony, either. Like it's a good thing. His wife was droning on. Humble-bragging. How *obsessive* she is about recycling. That she *obsesses* over washing and separating her, I don't know. Plastics. But she doesn't actually wash or separate sh—anything."

"No light housework, even," murmured Connie. "No bed making. No folding laundry or washing dishes. She won't even pick a toy or a book off the floor. Or tell her children to. The maids do it all for them. While she points. And then says, 'I'm so *obsessive.*'"

"So Connie goes, 'Hmm. A lifetime of recycling won't make up for a month of flying around in that private plane, though.'"

"I should never have said it," said Connie. "Very rude! I know! But at a certain point, not to engage is cowardly. Don't you think?"

"People default to cowardice," said Gil. "At least, *I* do."

"They say those who live in glass houses shouldn't throw stones," said Connie. "But don't we all?"

"Throw stones?" said Van Alsten.

"Live in glass houses," said Connie.

"Some houses are more glass than others," said Gil.

Connie regarded him thoughtfully, nodding. "But they can all be broken," she said.

A shiver ran through him.

The air-conditioning was frigid.

"Some guys would just cop to it, like yeah, I fly private, so sue me," said Van Alsten. "Not my brother. He had to have the last word. Rest of the holiday he was following us around jeering at everything we did like a six-year-old. Going, Are you sure you really want to eat that turkey? It has a *carbon footprint.* Are you sure you want to drive to the grocery store? That has a *carbon footprint.* You sure you need to use my Japanese toilet? It has a big—"

"We get it," said Connie.

"I wanted to punch his face in," said Van Alsten.

"I regretted speaking," said Connie. "But then, I often do."

"Know what you mean," said Gil. "It's safer not to. Typically."

The waiter appeared. "All right, folks, mix-and-match fajitas?"

"Thanks," said Van Alsten.

When Connie got up to go to the bathroom, Gil experienced a second of curiosity about her ass. Quelled it. With prejudice.

It was barely prurient, even. Could he be blamed for curiosity, when said ass was the stuff of myth and legend?

Anyway, her coat precluded any sighting.

He found himself tongue-tied, left alone with Van Alsten. Two men. Dullards. Blunt instruments.

Women made conversation easier.

He shook his glass. The ice cubes cracked and shifted.

"What?" asked Van Alsten.

"You're different when your wife's around."

"Of *course* I'm fucking different," said Van Alsten. "What do you take me for, a fool?"

"You're like a PG version of yourself."

"Connie brings out the best in me. Or whatever the fuck. She makes me a fucking better man."

"Until the second she leaves the room."

"Duh," said Van Alsten. "Still. I'm a better man at least sixty-five hours a week."

"A part-time good person?"

"Hey. You know what they say. In private, even Mother Teresa was an asshole."

When they were waiting for the check it was Van Alsten's turn to get up, and Gil was left with Connie.

A tag team.

"He doesn't like to express positive emotion," said Connie. "But you mean a lot to him. He used to look forward all week to going out with you and Vic. He said you two were civilians. Which, for him, can sometimes be a put-down. But in your case there's always been respect. He told me once you were civilians who still insisted on serving."

"Oh," said Gil.

"As few civilians do. He said."

A flush of warmth. He might have been blushing.

"Well. How *else* am I going to spend my time," he said.

"Paint pictures? Go to wine tastings in Napa Valley?"

"Ha. Well. No artistic talent. And I'm more the beer and whiskey type. But thank you."

She reached out and squeezed his hand.

"I'm glad you had a connection here," said Gil.

"Honestly? It was the only way he'd agree to the trip."

IN THE INTENSE HEAT more birds came to drink from the pond's waterfall. So many that they whitened the rocks, and the gardener took it upon himself to scrub them down.

Gil had hired him not because he didn't have the time to take care of the yard himself—hell, he had all the time in the world—but because he lacked the knowledge. He didn't want to kill the desert plants. But seeing the gardener kneeling, he remembered the guy had remarked he had joint problems. He was no spring chicken.

Decided to do that part himself, in the future. You didn't need plant expertise to scrub up bird shit.

Tom invited him to an aquarium in Scottsdale. The family were all going, so Gil said why not. Just in case, though, he'd drive his own car. He pictured mobs, screaming groups of children in matching day camp T-shirts. Needed an escape route.

But it was tranquil. Serene. In a blue tunnel where water wrapped around them, on either side and over their heads, they inspected the marine life of the Great Barrier Reef. The real reef, said a passing tour guide, had just been devastated by a mass bleaching event.

Butterflyfish and clownfish swam by.

"Oh!" exclaimed Ardis, behind him.

He turned: a dark-haired, slim woman. Ardis hugged her, then introduced her to Gil. Invited them both to lunch.

In the aquarium's cafeteria, he and Ted sat down at a table while the others lined up at the registers to order.

"I mentioned a lot of our friends had gotten divorced," said Ted. "Remember? She's one of them. She has a membership here. Likes to do paperwork on her laptop with the tanks around her and the fish swimming. Finds it relaxing."

Oddly, along with cheeseburgers and fries, the cafeteria served a Korean dish called bibimbap. Tom found the word hilarious. So he repeated it.

"Bibimbap, bibimbap, bibimbap. Bibimbap, bibimbap, bibim—"

"Shut *up*!" said Clem. "My *God*!"

Sarah sat down across from him with her tray.

"So Gil," she said, "how do you like our desert?"

Like Ardis, she was easy to talk to. His own replies were only moderately stilted. Once, laughing at something she had said, he caught sight of Ardis and Ted exchanging a look. Nothing wrong with it—a fond, satisfied look.

But was it complicit?

Driving home, he found he was agitated. The cloth of his shirt felt itchy. Was it a coincidence that a single woman had shown up?

He hoped there hadn't been any purpose behind the encounter. That it hadn't been an effort at matchmaking.

Because they felt sorry for him.

IN THE CASTLE there was a large skylight above a room his online real-estate agent had called "the atrium." It evoked a general idea of something ancient Roman. Mosaics made of small tiles lined the floors and walls, and columns were arrayed in a rectangle around a central garden.

He'd thought of Pompeii when he first saw it. Vesuvius. Mosaics covered in volcanic ash.

Over the garden was a patch of sky.

After the aquarium trip he set his sleeping pad beneath it. It was the pad he'd carried in his pack for all the months he walked—a grimy extension of his own body. He lay on the pad on his back.

Usually the city lights overwhelmed the stars. Or clouds blotted them out.

But on moonless nights, without much dust in the air, you could make out the constellation Perseus. And Venus, the bright planet.

There was a meteor shower in Perseus this time of year, so he lay there looking upward as his eyes adjusted, waiting to glimpse a shooting star.

He thought of the couples he knew. The world was all couples, after a certain age. Or looked that way, if you weren't in one.

Ted's friends might all be divorced, as he had claimed, but in fact Gil doubted it. More likely the remark had been an effort to comfort him. In his bachelorhood.

He was a lone satellite, orbiting. Ardis and Ted, Val Alsten and Connie, Rajiv and Amara, Vic and his kindly wife Inez.

Gazing at the blackness of the sky, he thought of them as well-fitting sets of creatures, nestled together for warmth. In the folds of each other's wings.

Who among them was lonely?

Maybe none.

But loneliness could be ambient, in a couple. Or get that way.

He'd pursued Lane, back in the day, with single-minded dedication. In their later years, whenever she seemed distant, he'd wondered if his early conviction had been a whim. And his unflagging pursuit of her like a form of weather.

A passing squall that had carried them both off and left them on a small island.

CUCKOOS

"MY NEW SCHOOL'S GONNA SUCK SO BAD," said Tom.

In the Southwest, school started early—at the beginning of August.

The two of them sat on the terrace drinking their different poisons, Gil a beer, Tom a soda.

It was near dusk, and the feathery shade of mesquite trees fell across the flagstones and cooled them. Gil had taken off his socks and shoes to feel the stone against his bare feet, stretched out his legs in front of the sagging canvas chair he sat in. Watched a roadrunner skedaddle across the ground and dip its head in the pond water.

He'd seen it catch a lizard that morning, the lizard's striped tail hanging limply from its beak.

In the yard, trees and shrubs moved in a warm breeze.

Then Tom had come running up the outside stairs and stated

that he was thirsty, so Gil had fetched him his favorite cola and sat down again.

Now his naked man-feet, previously unobserved, glared up at him whitely. He regretted that Tom had to witness such nudity.

Young children should be shielded from old feet.

"It's gonna suck? Why's that?" asked Gil.

"Clem heard the kids there *dab*," said Tom. He curled his lip in a sneer. "They still dab *now*! It's disgusting!"

"Dab?" said Gil.

"You don't know what *dabbing* is?"

"Should I?"

"*Everyone* knows, Gil. It's like the worst move ever *invented*. The worst dance move *ever*. I can't stand to show you. That's how cringe. It's so stupid and old that *no kids* do it anymore in Denver. In like *five years* nobody's dabbed."

"So what are you going to do? If *you* see someone dabbing?"

"I'd grab his arm, but not hurt him. I know! I'd put him in a wrist lock."

Tom would make plenty of kid friends in fifth grade, Gil thought.

Soon their golden age of play would end.

"I'm betting the school will grow on you," he said.

It wasn't till middle school that shit got real, if Gil remembered correctly from his own childhood. Tom should have another year's grace.

From fifth grade he clearly recalled one element only: color-coded cards in a cardboard file box, with a different nonfiction story on each card. They'd be outmoded by now, though. A card in the red section had been titled "Captain Cook Finds a New Land."

In the orange section, "Fun for the Otter Family."

He'd enjoyed reading the cards, making his way at high speed through the rainbow colors in the box.

He swiftly completed the questions on the back.

But his grandmother had died the summer after that, and he went to sixth grade more alone than ever.

Vicky D'Amato, who'd been held back a couple of years and was tall with large breasts like a shelf, had sat behind him in math. She'd tickled his back and he'd thought he would burn up. A searing, prickly heat.

After the tickling, Vicky followed him down the row of lockers jeering at him and giggling. He hadn't got the joke.

Even now he wasn't sure he got it.

LATER HE GOOGLED dabbing. Tom hadn't been wrong. It did look pretty bad.

WHEN THEY FIRST lived together, in a one-bedroom off Central Park West with narrow steps up to a roof garden, he and Lane inherited two tabby cats. Temporarily: part of the six-month sublet. The cats were a mandatory feature.

They were littermates but very different. One was smart and mean, hissing and swiping with its claws. The other was dumb and affectionate.

Their names were on the tags of their collars, but Lane ignored the tags. She called the dumb one Gil and the mean one Lane.

A PHOTO POPPED UP on his phone from an unknown number. Of Ardis and him at the aquarium. Their faces were arrayed in profile, eyes fixed on a tank in front of them.

The picture showed nothing in the tank but some long, slender reeds.

You were trying to find the seahorses, texted the unknown number. *The pregnant males with their sacs of eggs.*

Wait, who is this? he texted.

Sarah. Ardis's friend.

Ardis must have given her his cell.

He felt an anxious tug. It seemed like more evidence of social engineering. Geometry. As though he was being paired up.

He wasn't fit for it—he was compromised. He might not look that way to casual observers, but he was stricken.

Split between past and present. Less than whole.

Lane's memory took up the space where new affection might live. Lost and aimless, like a faithful dog.

Confused by the disappearance of its master.

HE SUSPECTED he hadn't been less intelligent than she was, though she'd liked to imply it, teasing him. He hadn't gone in for IQ tests the way she had—Lane enjoyed various forms of measurement and evaluation—but he had no direct evidence of a deficiency. He'd always done well in school.

But he'd been slower to make decisions, and Lane took his willingness to comply with her own decisions to be a weakness of analysis. She was competitive, while he was not. He didn't want to win.

He only wanted to be worthy.

When she came into a room his attention was always fixed on her. He liked the way she spoke. Her mannerisms and movements. The brackets around her mouth when she smiled, her high cheekbones, the way her clothes sat on her body. It didn't matter what clothes they were. She wore them all gracefully.

She danced around the apartment, half nude and giddy, to loud music. That was graceful too.

Lane observed both strangers and acquaintances with acute attention to detail. Maybe an upwelling of sympathy, maybe a sharp spur of condemnation. He saw other people through her eyes, and the double gaze illuminated them. She generated a sphere of purpose and cohesion around the two of them, and he liked being caught up in it. She was a singular force.

But she also had hard edges. Among them a strict policy of not apologizing after harsh words said in anger—at least, until he'd walked around for hours or days carrying a heavy rock of misery. He never said those harsh words. Only she did. And she was convinced of her own infallibility. Her judgments were always the right ones. The only ones.

In her mind she rode above the rest of the populace on a majestic steed. Possibly white. A stallion.

She could badger him for hours about the weaknesses she perceived in him, as though, simply by listing his defects repeatedly, she might one day obliterate them.

Despite those edges, which only grew harder with time, he'd clung to her. Right up to the end, he'd never allowed for the possibility of an ending.

So in a way—he'd recognized it even then—the dumb cat had been well named.

And maybe the mean one too.

AFTER HIS SHIFT was done, the evening of the day Tom and Clem started school, Lori invited him to sit in the common room with a group of guests.

He was tired and couldn't think fast enough to make an excuse. He said, Thank you, just for a few minutes. I'm not supposed to fraternize. And I have to be somewhere soon.

He had to be home. Doing nothing.

When he walked into the room he was more conscious than usual of being male. It struck him he might be the only man left in the building. One man inside the fortress of the hurt women.

They must have put the children to bed. They sat on couches in the semi-dark of a few table lamps.

"This one wedding I went to," said one of them, "the maid of honor was a guy."

"What. A guy in drag?"

"No. Just a guy."

"This friend of mine had a Ren Faire wedding," said another one. Young and maybe new—he didn't recognize her. "She was a duchess and the maids of honor were ladies-in-waiting. She made us all dress like, medieval. I had to go as a serving wench. With those like, ties up the front? But three months later she went off her meds. He wanted kids so she went off the meds. And that was it. Divorce."

An older woman spoke from a blur of blue clothing in a corner chair. Denim. Her face was in shadow.

"Better than your story," she said. "At least she didn't stay married to a guy who talked with his fists."

"Um," said the young woman, wounded. "Have faith that he can change? That's what my pastor said."

The denim woman guffawed. "There's faith and there's stupidity."

"She's not calling *you* stupid, honey," another woman said, and leaned over to pat the young one's hand.

"I'm not?" said the blue woman.

"What do you think, Gil?" asked Lori, deflecting. "Does *anyone* mean it when they promise to change?"

On the spot. Not a fit position for him.

He represented the violent male. His was the voice of the aggressor.

The others turned and looked at him.

"My opinion? It doesn't matter."

"Say what you think. Don't be dickless," said the blue woman.

"What I was saying was just that, in my opinion, whether he means it or not doesn't matter," said Gil evenly.

You had to stay calm if a guest called you names. Calm was the key.

"Fuckin' A," said the blue woman. She was nodding, but he wasn't sure what fuckin' A meant.

"My personal feeling is, don't hang around to find out," he said.

"What *he* said," nodded the blue woman.

She reminded him of a truck driver. Long haul.

He'd met a lot of truckers on the long walk. Truck-stop diners had been his salvation. When he'd been sleeping at rest areas or on the edge of culverts between distantly spaced motels, subsisting on packets of tuna and powdered noodle soup, a truck stop looming up in front of him had looked like paradise. He'd felt compelled by it, picking up his pace. Sat down gratefully in a counter or booth. Some of the diners had table service.

He'd ordered whatever greasy, warm food was on the menu. Waffles. Pancakes. Chicken-fried steak. Thrilled, he'd consumed it ravenously.

He'd generally found the truckers to be gruff and friendly, but a few were lunatics. One named Arnaldo claimed to have eaten only white items for the past ten years: rice, white bread, vanilla ice cream, milk.

Gil asked what he did about vegetables. Didn't he need to eat a few? For health reasons?

Well, cauliflower, sometimes, said Arnaldo. But mostly it was potatoes that kept him going. Mashed. If he found even a bit of brown peel, though, he refused to eat those mashed potatoes.

Sent them right back to the hellhole they came from.

The cab of his truck was white also, both inside and out, and so were his clothes. He believed the answer to everything was white.

He'd told Gil this and then said, "So ask me, what's the question? Go on, ask. What is the question if the answer is always white?"

Gil was afraid to find out. He changed the subject to lactose intolerance.

Among the truckers there were also a fair number of conspiracy hacks. Most of the theories Gil had heard before. A guy from Georgia said he'd never have an operation. Because the doctors put computer chips in you. So that the government could track your movements.

9/11 was also a theme. There too, the feds had been the evil masterminds.

In the wake of the election, he heard even more conspiracies. Words like *cabal* were used.

"Fool me once, shame on you," said the blue woman now, to the young one. "Fool me twice, shame on me."

HE HADN'T BEEN the only man in the building, in fact, because as he left he converged with Jason at the staff entrance.

Jason made conversation as they walked across the street to their cars, asking what part of town Gil lived in. Gil said he had a big yard beside a wash on public parkland, and many wild birds came through.

For instance, there was a pair of roadrunners, he told Jason, raising his fob and clicking his car open. The crests on top of their heads rose and flexed like a hand's worth of fingers.

"True fact: they're in the cuckoo family," said Jason.

"Is that right. Roadrunners are cuckoos?"

"And they mate for life."

Jason saluted awkwardly and got into his minivan.

Driving home, Gil thought how people liked to say that about other animals. They mate for life, said people in smug admiration.

As though this lifelong mating was a prudent, morally upright trait that showed great sexual restraint.

A trait some few, superior species among the rest of the animals were fortunate enough to share with their betters, humans.

But humans didn't do it much anymore. The shelter's director had told him the global divorce rate was 44 percent. And rising.

Let's get divorced! said couples everywhere, excited.

Hearing her statistic had allowed him to derive a faint relief over the usually dismal fact that he had never married.

He'd wanted to, but Lane had not.

"SO HOW'S SCHOOL TREATING YOU?" he asked Tom, in the glass house living room.

Tom shrugged and got shifty-eyed. Gil had come over to see if he wanted to skateboard, since the sky was overcast, the sun hidden. A metallic silver.

He thought Tom was pale. Was that it? Tom looked different. He couldn't put his finger on it.

In the end Tom said yes, he'd come out.

But he was quiet as he coasted around. His shoulders slumped. Gil didn't push him. They both tried to pass it off as normal.

WARNING SIGNS of depression in children, said one of the webpages he looked at. Social withdrawal. Fatigue. Low energy.

With all the hours he'd spent depressed as a boy, he shouldn't have needed to resort to a search engine.

But seeing the list was halfway reassuring. Many line items didn't match Tom's affect.

It was a new school, after all.

ARDIS KNOCKED at the sliding door to the terrace. She held a small pitcher in her hand, the pitcher she used to pour sugar water into the bird feeder.

He opened the door and invited her in, but she said she had food on the stove, so he stepped out onto the flagstones himself.

"Hey. You're not in the mood for dating, are you," she said, as she unhooked the empty feeder from its branch.

He made an *enh* sound and lifted his shoulders. That was one way of putting it, he guessed.

"I *know*," she said, sympathetic. "Nobody's business but yours. I didn't try to set you up, I promise. I didn't know Sarah would be there. At the aquarium. I didn't plan for us to meet that day. And then she just took to you."

He didn't know what to say. It wasn't Sarah. She was likable. A warm and accomplished person. Impressive, even. A surgeon.

Also, she had a slender neck. Well-shaped shoulders. She was very pretty, in fact.

"I mean. With her, specifically, I'd worry . . ." he started. "I'd worry about complications. Missteps. You know—hurt feelings. Triangulation."

When he was earnest, he was inarticulate.

"I understand," said Ardis. "I really do."

"Because you're my neighbors," he added. "But also my friends."

"Yes. We are."

She gave him a quizzical glance, half sad. Then reached out and lightly grasped his wrist.

The look changed from wistful to something he couldn't quite pin down.

She turned to leave.

"You can do your best and still fail," he said after a minute, to her back. She was already at the bottom of the stairs, likely too distant to hear. "You can do your best all your life."

He hadn't planned to say it.

He kicked off his flip-flops inside the sliding door and plodded into his den, at loose ends. Opened a file cabinet and fished out an envelope. Looked at pictures of his mother and father, himself as an infant and a toddler.

He'd never put them into albums—when his parents died he'd been too young for that, then later he'd been too old.

So they rested in a manila envelope.

There he was in a family portrait. His mother and father were young and wore seventies plaids, both with dark-brown hair and clean-looking faces. He was chubby-cheeked. Possibly four. The photo might have been taken near the time of the accident.

Its background was a cold, fake-sky blue.

He studied their eyes and mouths the way he always had— their eyes aimed over the photographer's head, their smiles. The small boy between them was unsmiling.

He thought what he always thought when he took out the pictures: that he'd never know them.

Behind the faces were strangers.

He mulled over what he'd said to Ardis's back. *Do your best all your life.* What was that? Nothing but self-pity.

All it meant was, you expected some surprising change, some exciting reversal, while being exactly who you'd always been.

He pictured crowds hunkered down. Committed. Being themselves with dogged perseverance.

But all the while they hoped to be interrupted by an unexpected event—deliverance.

They dreamed of being lifted up. Being swung out in giddy delight over glittering peaks.

Aloft in the sparkling air.

MISTLETOE

HE WATCHED TOM come home in the afternoons, walking up the street from the school-bus stop. A bulky, sagging pack hung off his back, his thin shoulders bent under its weight.

His posture had changed. He dragged his feet when he walked. Disappeared for long periods into his bedroom. In the backyard his punching bag hung from its tree unused, its red vinyl bleaching to pink and cracking in the sun.

He wondered what Ardis was thinking. She must have noticed. She must be concerned too.

But he couldn't bring himself to ask. Couldn't quite say, Your son seems depressed to me.

He wasn't a therapist. Or even a parent.

Doubly unqualified.

Still something ached in him when he looked at Tom. He

dreamed about it. In one dream a little boy was mixed up with a bird. The lower half of his body dwindled into bird-shape, human legs missing.

In another Tom grew thinner and thinner, surrounded by a crowd of other boys. The crowd expanded until Gil couldn't see him anymore.

HE SPOTTED SOME new, unfamiliar birds on the very tops of trees. Silhouetted. The males were jet black with crests on their heads, while the females were an ashy gray.

They survived on a single berry, Jason said, when Gil described the birds to him.

Jason was an avid birdwatcher.

The red berries were the fruit of a species called dwarf mistletoe, he said. Gil had seen it in his yard: an olive-green mass of wiry stems that bubbled up like tussocks on the branches of native trees.

After the birds ate the berries, they excreted the seeds onto the branches of other trees. This was how the mistletoe reproduced.

Without the birds the mistletoe would die off, and without the mistletoe so might the birds.

Phainopepla, was the name of the bird.

Some gardeners said mistletoe was a parasite that should be ripped out before it killed its hosts, Jason told him. Others said to leave it.

They said the birds and trees and mistletoe lived in a complex symbiosis. That had lasted for thousands of years.

MAYBE TOM NEEDED a distraction, Gil decided. And went to find him. He was in the glass house living room by himself, playing a console game.

His thumbs worked the controller. On the screen a skateboarding avatar soared into the air and fell hard in a concrete bowl.

A red X-ray image flashed up. The avatar's broken bones. An ankle was snapped in half. And a femur.

"Ow," said Gil. "Graphic." He winced.

"I mean, but not like a *shooter*," said Tom. "I'm not allowed first-person shooters."

"I heard."

"It's dumb. I asked them why and they said ideation. It means getting ideas."

"Right, yeah. Shooting ideas, I guess?"

"What do they think? I'm going to play a game and then turn into one of those crazy school-killer guys?"

"I think it's more like, you'll imagine stuff too often. From the shooter position. You know, violent imagery. What people say is, the images themselves aren't great. To have in your head a lot."

"It's dumb." Tom shook his head.

"I have a favor to ask," said Gil.

"What." Monotone.

"I was wondering if you could teach me to skateboard."

"You want to learn how to *skate*?"

Tom was surprised enough to look up.

"I mean. I'm way too old to take lessons from pros. It'd be humiliating."

Tom went back to his toggling.

"I have an extra board," he said after a minute. "But my helmet wouldn't fit you."

Gil said he could use his bike helmet.

Tom talked about tricks. Pop shove-its, ollies. Gil said he'd break his neck if he tried those. He was forty-five! He just wanted to master pushing.

So they strapped on their gear and Tom led him into the cul-de-sac.

A neighbor Gil didn't know was parking her car in her driveway. She glared at them as she carried in groceries. Blond hair in a frizzy square.

Tom showed Gil how to put his feet on the board.

"Left foot on the back's called goofy," he instructed. "Most people aren't goofy. *You're* not goofy."

"Might be a matter of opinion."

Usually Tom laughed at his lame remarks. Not today.

"I mean your left foot's first."

"How's school?" Gil asked, trying to balance.

"OK," said Tom. But his face closed. "Um. Keep your back foot on the screws."

The neighbor woman was outside again, slamming the back door of her SUV. She turned and glared at them again.

"Hey, hi!" called Gil, though it went against every fiber of his being. He stepped off the board awkwardly, and it rolled and slowly hit the curb. "I'm Gil. The old house on the rise there. This is Tom. He lives next door, in the glass one."

"I've seen you doing this before. But it's against the rules," she said peevishly.

"The rules?"

"The bylaws? The neighborhood association?"

"Ah," said Gil.

He hadn't read them. Left the documents to the lawyers.

"Skateboarding is a violation of the bylaws."

"Oh. Is it bothering you?"

"The point is, it's a *community*," she said. "And we have rules."

She was getting on his nerves.

"There's a rule about basketball hoops, too," said Tom to Gil. "You can't have one in the driveway."

"I see," said Gil. He turned back to the woman. "Sorry. I didn't catch your name?"

"Ellen."

"Ellen. It's good to meet you. Listen, I didn't have the rules down. That's on me. Ignorance of the law is no excuse. I'll get up to speed. But is this harming you? Because it's great for us. Just to come out here. There's hardly any traffic. You know?"

The woman crossed her arms over her chest.

"I don't feel like you're *hearing* me," she said.

It was a standoff.

"Let's go in," said Tom, under his breath. "It's wrecked now anyway. She wrecked it."

They picked up their boards and went.

"It's a *community*," mimicked Tom as they stepped onto Gil's driveway.

Gil smiled, conflicted. Supposedly, the young should be taught to respect rules. Yet here he was. Schooling young Tom in disrespect.

Still. He wished Van Alsten had been there. Ready to use his foul mouth.

"My bad," he said, "I didn't know the rule."

"The rule's mean," said Tom. "And that lady is too."

"Hey. We'll figure it out. A skate park, maybe. I know you're intimidated by the older guys. I get it. But maybe I can find us an empty one."

ONE YEAR, when he and Lane were still in their twenties, they'd sent out a holiday form letter instead of cards. She'd been chronically irritated by all the long, tedious Christmas letters they got from her large extended family.

It had become a tradition for her to read the worst passages aloud. In-depth accounts of children's activities in sports, with details of the games. Blow-by-blow accounts of home redecorations. Three paragraphs on a great-aunt's bunion operation, with before-and-after pictures. A list of the performances of a folk-dancing group in Appalachia. The résumé of a teen cousin who shone as brightly as the sun.

Four elite colleges had embraced him, the letter said. And named each one. Also, the Young Republicans.

They'd written their own form letter together. Over most of a bottle of wine for Lane and two cocktails for him.

Dear friends and family, it read. *This year we did not get engaged. We acquired no pet, and we did not produce a child. We did not buy a car or house. We did not take the package deal. We did not join the club. We did not order the special. We never multiplied our miles.*

We had some arguments, that's true.

*There was so much we did not see. We did not know. We did not
understand.*

At times we drank heavily.

Happy holidays to all! xoo, Lane and Gil.

The letter had not been well received.

VAN ALSTEN called him. He didn't notice it at first because he
got so few voicemails he'd stopped checking them. By the time he
saw it and listened and called, a day had passed.

"Connie's sick," said Van Alsten.

"Sick how?"

Van Alsten said she needed a kidney. Surprisingly, he had
proved to be a match. So he was going to give her one.

His kidneys weren't in mint condition, he said. But they were
all she had.

She hadn't let the kids be tested, even. Although they'd both
offered.

Those were some good kids, thought Gil.

"I didn't realize she had health problems," he said.

"She doesn't like me to talk about them," said Van Alsten.

AN ANGRY MAN came to the shelter. Lori's husband, the
bearlike veteran. She'd forgotten to turn off the locator on her
phone.

And he wanted his dog back.

The shelter didn't allow pets, so the dog was staying with a friend. Possibly the husband did not know this. When Lori and her daughter left their home they'd also moved the dog. He'd kicked it, and it had two broken ribs.

The husband wept in the yard. He wept and shouted, shouted and wept. He said he hadn't meant to hurt his dog. He said the dog was all he had left.

Please, please, please, please, he said. He would never hurt his dog again.

Gil watched from a window with Lori, while others kept the children busy in the playroom. There was a policy calling for guests and staff to remain inside the locked building and wait for the police, but he found he had a strong desire to go outside. Had to work to suppress it.

He wanted to take the bearlike man by his shoulders and say, I'm sorry you had to fight in a war. I'm sorry you broke your dog's ribs. I'm sorry for everything.

When the man's energy was spent he sat down on the dried grass. Buried his face in his hands. A cruiser pulled up with its lights flashing but no siren.

It was a residential neighborhood, and the shelter had requested discretion.

They bundled him into the backseat and drove away.

ARDIS DECIDED TO throw a housewarming party. Gil was impressed she knew enough people to invite, considering that they'd just moved from Colorado.

Mostly colleagues. From both their offices, said Ted.

Before the party Ardis had to get permission for street parking from the neighborhood association. She also had to warn the neighbors. She persuaded Gil and Tom to make the rounds with her, telling the neighbors that noise would happen. And many cars would be parking.

Also inviting them, she said.

"Do we have to invite the mean lady?" asked Tom.

"The meaner they are, the more we have to invite them," said Ardis.

"That's not fair," said Tom.

"But strategic," said his mother.

They went from door to door, and when the neighbors weren't home Tom slid an invitation under their doors.

JASON WAS BEHAVING erratically, the staff muttered. He started missing shifts, calling too late for substitutes to be brought in. Except for Gil, who always said yes at the last minute.

Or he arrived hours too early and hung out in the kitchen, consuming the shelter's painstakingly budgeted groceries.

He'd been volunteering for two years. Reliable. The coordinator was reluctant to take action.

"Maybe you could talk to him," she said. "Unofficially?"

"I don't know how to talk *officially*," said Gil. "So that should work."

Jason was at the kitchen table with an open loaf of bread. He was busy spreading peanut butter on three pieces.

"Hungry," said Jason.

"A man needs to eat," allowed Gil.

Maybe he could focus on the man aspect. With being men, they had an element in common.

But nothing in that genre occurred to him.

Jason picked up his first piece of slathered bread and started to nibble it around the crust, rotating it rapidly until all the crust was gone.

"So those black birds, what did you say they were? The ones that eat the mistletoe berries?"

"Phainopeplas," said Jason with his mouth full.

"OK, yeah. I knew it was a big word."

"*Phainopepla nitens*," said Jason. "Attractive eggs. Pink and speckled."

He folded the de-crusted bread into a smaller square and tucked the package into his mouth. His cheeks pouched out as he chewed.

"Have you been getting out much?" asked Gil. "You like to go birding down south, right? What was your favorite spot again? Madera Canyon?"

"I can't," said Jason. "Susan won't let me."

"Susan?"

"My sister."

"Your sister won't let you travel?"

"She makes me watch our mother all the time."

"You're looking after your mother?"

"Paralyzed. From a stroke."

"I'm sorry. Very tough," said Gil.

"She won't let me put her in assisted living," he said, through the nibbling. "She says it's elder abuse."

"Does your sister help too?" said Gil.

"She lives in Indiana," said Jason.

"Oh."

"I'm only allowed out for work," said Jason. He was a computer programmer. "And stuff like this. Community service. A caregiver comes."

"Wow. Strict rules, for a grown person."

"And Susan put cameras in the house."

"Cameras?"

"To make sure I don't bring home ladies."

His mother was an observant Mormon, he said. She'd be disturbed if he had unmarried women in the house with them.

Gil thought for a minute.

"That sounds wrong."

Jason chewed. Tears came out of his eyes.

"Listen," said Gil. "I think maybe you need to change your situation. Change it up a bit."

"I *can't*!" said Jason, swallowing. He choked, then got a handle on it. "I can't! She won't let me!"

"We're gonna work on this," said Gil. "OK? We'll talk it through."

Jason nodded.

"I think you got your protein," said Gil. "And your carbs. Good work. Let's go sit for a minute. Here. I'll put the loaf away for you."

LANE HAD BROKEN UP with him twice. The first time, only a couple of years in, he'd left the city afterward. And the state and country.

Flight. A dry run for later, he saw now.

He let her keep living in their apartment—Hadley, his money manager, had told him to invest in Manhattan real estate, so he'd bought one after the sublet—and flew down to the Amazon.

He liked the sound of it. The jungle had a certain reputation.

There he slept in a tent on a wooden platform and helped the locals, and some well-meaning hippies from Vermont, on a small organic farming and ecotourism project. Along with other similar projects, their mixed-use farming and forest-product harvesting model was supposed to dissuade people from slashing and burning the Ecuadorian rainforest. To raise cattle for burgers.

It did not.

A "sustainable alternative to forest liquidation," he heard one of the Vermonters tell the visiting CEO of a fast-food company.

The CEO coughed into his hand, hiding a smirk.

He'd flown in on a chopper. With a video crew to document his outreach activities.

For the more liberal among the shareholders.

In the rainforest, Gil had no cell phone service and no laptop. He worked on composting systems and planting. Some days he was assigned to trail maintenance, chopping his way through the greenery with a dull machete. That was the worst assignment. He wore a net over his face, but mosquitoes plagued him.

He was wet all the time, and filmy with sweat and dirt. To take a shower, he hung a bag of water from a tree, punctured the plastic with a utility knife, and stood beneath it.

At night he often fell asleep in his tent early, while the Vermonters sang around the campfire. He must have heard a hundred renditions of "This Land Is Your Land." Sometimes he got choked up as he listened.

Other times he wished they would find a new song.

He seldom dreamed but tossed and turned, waking up early to the deafening buzz of cicadas that sounded like lawn mowers.

He saw beetles as long as his hand and once a so-called wandering spider. The locals said their venom could cause long-lasting erections. Which led to impotence.

He was not bitten.

Every week a volunteer would fetch the mail, delivered to a town an hour away by riverboat. After a few months he got a letter from Lane.

She had reconsidered. He could come home, if he wanted.

He stayed another month for good measure: he had his pride.

By then he'd gotten used to the mosquito bites, and even the cicadas he barely heard anymore.

But eventually he went back to her.

ARDIS'S PARTY WAS well attended.

He brought over some food, tofu skewers with peanut sauce, grilled vegetables, and samosas he'd learned to make from Rajiv.

At Tom's request, he was trying not to cook meat. To help the animals, Tom said, and lower their carbon footprint. Beef was the worst, Tom lectured. Fifteen percent of greenhouse gas emissions, he told them. At least.

He helped her and Ted set up, then went home to bathe and change. Freshly clothed, he stuck his head out his front door: parked cars lined the street.

One of them he recognized—Jason's minivan. It was notable for its logjam of bird-related bumper stickers.

And there was the man himself, jogging up the front walk.

"I did it!" he said, arriving at the door breathless.

He bent down and braced his hands on his knees, huffing and puffing, then straightened. He wore a bright-red T-shirt with a pair of brown binoculars on it and the words CAN'T TALK NOW I'M BIRDING. Also a nylon fanny pack.

"You did it?" said Gil.

He had no idea how Jason had gotten his address.

"I found a place for my mother!" said Jason.

At the bar Jason accepted a near-beer, which Gil kept on hand out of an old barkeeping habit.

Though Jason was only a jack Mormon, he said, he'd kept the habit of not drinking.

He told of the facility he'd found. It had an indoor swimming pool. And a shuttle that made field trips.

"And your sister. How's she taking it?"

"She's not talking to me," said Jason.

He was keyed up. Defiant, he'd turned off the cameras.

"Well. OK. Breathing room," said Gil.

He couldn't ditch Jason. Not in his moment of triumph.

"My neighbors are having a party," he said. He put down his drink and walked out onto the terrace, Jason following. Instantly the sounds of talk and laughter swelled.

The glass house was teeming—it looked like an airport gate lounge.

"That one. You want to come with me?"

So Jason came to the party, near-beer and fanny pack included.

Sidling past guests to grab a beer, Gil thought he could guess who the colleagues were: dressed to impress, men in jackets and women in long dresses. The neighbors were in more casual getup. One guy wore sandals and Bermuda shorts.

The groups gathered in cliques, not mixing.

"Gil, hey," said someone.

It was Sarah, squeezing her way between neighbors.

She smiled, holding a glass of something pale yellow. Lemonade. Or a margarita.

He was surprised. Surprisingly glad she was there.

Had to remind himself what he already knew: that her appeal belonged in a compartment. And did not involve him.

Jason stood close, pressing into his side. A wingman with no confidence.

"This is Jason," he told Sarah. "We volunteer at the shelter together. He dropped by."

Jason switched hands on the near-beer to shake.

"Crowded in here," said Sarah to both of them. "I feel like I have to yell to be heard. Let's get you some finger food and check out the backyard."

On the back deck older kids stood around, awkwardly silent— Clem and three other teenage girls, who all wore crop tops above their jeans. They matched. Skinny and overly made up, with black lip liner and purple lips. As they leaned back against the wooden rail, their bare, concave stomachs caught the light. Foregrounded. They led with their stomachs.

The girls scrolled on phones in glittering, rhinestone-studded cases. Clem didn't seem to know them.

"Gil!" she said.

It had to be the happiest she'd ever been to see him.

"This is Clem," he told Jason. "She lives here. Clem, Jason, from my work. That I don't get paid for."

Clem flicked her eyes away from Jason. Took Gil by the arm and pulled him aside, leaning in close.

"I don't know what to *do*," she said, quiet and desperate. "I'm supposed to like, *entertain* them. What can we even *do*?"

He thought for a second. "You could walk them over to my house, if you want. There are some pinball machines in the basement. I collected them when I was younger."

In college, it had been. His one extravagance in the four years after his first meeting with the trustees. Something about the colorfulness of the machines, how different they were from the gray house of his childhood. With their sound and light, they'd been like parties he could own.

He and Rajiv had played them in their rented house off-campus, junior and senior year. Late at night with a lot of beer.

"Oh. I don't *know*," said Clem.

"I'll make the offer. If they're not into it, I'll look like the idiot. Not you. Give me a minute. So it seems spontaneous."

Jason was telling Sarah about seasonal migrations. He pointed out the wash behind the yards and called it a "minor flyway."

Sarah listened politely. Said she was an animal lover herself. When she was little, she'd dreamed of being a marine biologist. But she failed at that—somehow she got sidetracked. And ended up a surgeon.

Jason nodded solemnly. Acknowledging her failure.

Once Clem was scrolling on her phone alongside the other girls, Gil announced his basement had a couple of amenities. There was a mini-fridge with drinks and snacks. And if anyone played pinball, there were vintage machines. Three from the eighties. One with William Shatner's face on it.

"Who's William *Shatner*?" said a girl with a nose diamond. Challenging.

"The *Star Trek* actor? Who played Captain Kirk?" said Gil.

She stared at him blankly.

"That doughy guy. From the Priceline commercials," added Sarah.

Still blank.

Another girl said pinball was kind of all right. Better than *nothing*, anyway. So where was his basement?

"Clem, could you take them over?"

She barely smiled, but still: mission accomplished.

"Wait," he said, as they were leaving. "You seen Tom anywhere?"

She shook her head. Otherwise occupied.

He braved the inside of the house again, threading his way through the crowds. In the kitchen he saw Ellen, who was opposed to skateboarding, gnawing on the side of a tofu skewer like it was a corncob.

Went into the core, toward Tom's bedroom. Knocked on the door. No answer.

"Hey, Tom? It's just me. Gil. Are you in there?"

When the door opened Tom had his earbuds in, dangling but unattached. He wore a hunted look.

"I was hoping you'd join the party," said Gil. "I'll keep the mean lady away from you."

Tom shook his head.

"It's not that."

"No? Then what is it?"

"I mean. I don't feel like it."

But Tom had made signs for the party. BATHROOM →. CLEM'S ROOM X PRIVATE PLEASE NO ENTRY.

He'd looked forward to hosting. He liked to give home tours. Show people things.

"Is something else bothering you?"

Tom retreated into his room. Gil stepped in and closed the door behind him.

"This kid is here," mumbled Tom. "This kid from the school bus."

"Is he a problem?"

Tom was uncomfortable. Shoulders hunched. Squirrely.

"He *does* stuff."

"What stuff? You can tell me."

"Like first he kicked my seat. He was behind. But really hard. He kept on doing it. I'd be, the whole ride, jiggling."

"Did you ask him to stop?"

"I *tried*. But he just smiled at me. Then he did rubber bands. Flicking them really hard. On my head."

"Did you tell the bus driver?"

"Clem says tattling's for losers. And *you* said it."

"I did?"

"You said it was beneath me. Telling on people."

Shit.

"Tom. I shouldn't have said it that simply. I was just talking about you and Clem. The brother-sister thing."

"Then he did paper clips. He uncurls them. He jabs them in."

He bent his head and pulled down his hoodie, exposing the back of his neck.

Large clusters of angry red punctures. Puffy skin. Pus.

They were badly infected.

"*Damn*, Tom!"

"Wherever I sit, he sits behind me. He gets on the bus right after me. In the morning. It's pretty empty then. If I move he follows me. Sometimes he jabs them in the holes he already put there. That hurts the most. One time I like, screamed."

"We're going to take care of those. And him."

"He lives near. We must have *invited* him!"

"Did you tell your parents?"

"They're *busy*. And you *said* not to tattle."

This was where the rubber hit the road. The danger of Gil's substitute parenting.

"You have to tell them, OK? And we need to put something on those puncture wounds. An antibiotic. I'll get you some from the medicine cabinet."

Tom nodded. Reluctant.

"Do you know his name?"

He shook his head.

"Show him to me. Come out and show me."

"What if he sees?"

"I've got your back."

Slowly Tom pulled out his earbuds and tossed them onto his bed.

They made their way into the open plan. The crowd had spilled into the backyard.

"He's not in here," mumbled Tom.

They stood on the back porch. Tom did a quick intake of breath.

"There. *There*," he said, and tipped his head.

Under the tree, a kid was punching his bag.

Not a hulk, just a kid.

"OK," said Gil. "You can go inside again. I'll be back soon. To get the antibiotic."

He went down the stairs and strolled across the grass.

"Hey," he said to the kid. "I'm Gil. Friend of the family. What's your name?"

"Brad," said the kid sullenly.

"Brad. You like martial arts?"

"Nah," said the kid.

"Tom does," said Gil. "The little guy who lives here. That's his bag. He's ten years old. How old are you?"

"Thirteen."

"You know who Tom is?"

The kid shook his head, kept punching.

"He's the one from the bus. The one whose neck you've been sticking paper clips into."

The kid stopped mid-punch. A long beat. Then he started to punch again.

That was a tip-off. If Gil hadn't already been sure.

Tom embellished the facts routinely, but Gil had never heard him tell an outright lie.

"That's gonna stop, though," said Gil. "Right away. This is your chance. Before the shit hits the fan. Got it? He doesn't want to turn you in. He doesn't want to be that guy. I happened to see the punctures, is what happened. I made him tell me how they got there. But you know how schools are about bullying. Zero tolerance, right? So from now on, bus or school or wherever, you don't sit behind him. Or anywhere near. You keep on walking, Brad. I mean it."

The *shit* was regrettable. Unlike Van Alsten, he tried to watch his language around kids.

But it had been called for, he decided.

Impact was needed. In the situation.

Turned and went back to the house.

HE DIDN'T LIKE to remember the second time Lane broke up with him, but there were moments when he couldn't help it. Late at night, when he was trying to fall asleep.

He'd been volunteering about sixty hours a week at a food bank in Queens, and she worked long hours at her job. She'd fought her way up through the ranks and was a senior editor at a glossy magazine owned by a media conglomerate. It sold the outdoors.

Or outdoor activities, anyway: rock-climbing adventures, triathlons, Everest expeditions. Extreme sports and high-end sporting gear.

She spent a lot of time with celebrity athletes, wining and dining them for interviews. She and Gil barely saw each other. He would try to pin her down for an occasional evening, but she was always too busy.

One morning, after she left for work, he'd decided to make a plea. They had to rein this in, living alongside each other without touching. He missed her. Couldn't they be lighthearted again?

Collections of videos popped up in his inbox from photo services they'd used. "Ten years ago today." He'd recorded her a lot, back when she'd let him. Taunting him and smiling when they were alone. Conversations with their friends. There was one he particularly liked of her skiing along a city street in swirling snow during a blizzard.

They'd skied together with free-sample cross-country skis she brought home from the office. Neither of them was skilled, but he'd been clumsier than she was and given up on speed. Lagged behind, filming her.

They'd ended up in their favorite neighborhood bar, skis propped up beside the door. Drank and ate bar food as the snow kept falling silently outside the window.

But he had to hit the trash button. He couldn't bear to look at the footage. It almost hurt his skin.

Now she was all business. What did she need? he would ask her. Whatever she needed, he was ready to furnish it.

He got home that night and found her possessions gone. A couple of pieces of furniture and small appliances, also. An antique chair, an espresso maker he'd thought was extravagant. A small sculpture she'd chosen and he'd bought.

On the coffee table where it had sat there was a note under a set of keys—her keys to the apartment.

It said three hackneyed words. *I met someone.*

She'd been biding her time for fifteen years. Waiting to meet someone.

PIGEON

HE TOLD ARDIS about Brad, and she took it in stride. She would resolve the problem without involving the school authorities, she said.

She'd met his mother at the party. A quiet woman with an overbearing husband. She would talk to her.

Ardis was even-keeled.

Ted not so much. He came over while Gil was packing and said he hadn't been there for Tom. Gil knew more about his son's inner life than he did.

"You work for a living, is all," said Gil, apologetic. "I'm just a parasite. I have time for everything."

"Don't run yourself down," said Ted, and poured himself a drink. "You're the nicest parasite I know."

"High praise indeed," said Gil.

He thought of the phainopeplas and the mistletoe. Maybe he should see his role as more symbiotic.

"Hey. Do you think Ardis could be having an affair?"

"Say *what?*"

The question actually shocked him.

"Just hypothetically."

"Ted. Why would you say that? Who would be married to you and have an affair? Plus, it's *Ardis.*"

"I had one once."

"You *did?*"

Ted nodded. "We got married right out of college. I cheated on her a couple of years after. Looking back, I was a dumb kid. It was a dumb choice. A dancer I saw three times. I told Ardis back then, and she forgave me."

So Ardis *had* been hurt. Like everyone else. Once, at least. But had risen above it.

"Maybe she wants an affair of her own," said Ted. "To balance it out."

"Is that how it works?"

"Shit, I don't know. It could, right? It'd only be fair. It could."

"I mean. How are things? Aren't things good?"

"They're pretty good. Yeah. At least, I think?"

"Then why the question?"

"It's just a hypothetical."

"My ex had an affair," said Gil. "Left me for him, in fact."

"Well, shit," said Ted.

"A famous cyclist. His calves were like iron."

"Me, personally? I don't like that look," said Ted. And shook his head. Closely resembled Tom, for an instant. "Those bunched-up muscles? Split in the middle, like two halves of some weird muscle-fruit? Creepy. Robotic. That's some *Terminator* shit right there."

"Thanks very much," said Gil. "Thank you for your support."

"Not a problem."

He hadn't known where Lane moved to. Her mail was automatically forwarded.

For a few weeks he didn't know who someone was, either.

Lane's friends had become his friends, too. But they'd been hers first and stuck with her. A couple didn't approve, possibly, but they had a noninterference policy. Apologetic but firm. They'd known Lane longer. And it wasn't as if the two of them had been *married*.

Because they hadn't been married, her betrayal was less serious. More of a gray area, maybe.

There were a few calls. And then the friends disappeared.

A woman had stopped by to pick up a few belongings Lane hadn't taken when she left. She was a work friend, an assistant.

Gil figured it was because of her subordinate status that she'd felt she had to accept the task. When he saw her discomfort, his anger began to dissipate. He invited her to call Lane, tell her she could have anything.

She made the call, and they piled more objects by the door. A tapestry he'd got for Lane on a trip they took to Morocco for her work. A food processor. A set of knives.

He offered the coworker a beer. She asked for another and got more comfortable. He rummaged through closets and tossed his own things out of boxes to make them available.

After a while she told him the name. He didn't have to ask. He wasn't familiar with it, not being a follower of the cycling circuit, but he looked it up after she left. He knew how to use a search engine.

The guy was a well-known hawker of carbon-fiber road bikes. They retailed around fifteen thousand dollars. His image could be seen on billboards. He'd once won the Tour de France.

"I'm not that paranoid," said Ted. "By nature. But. She seems so distracted."

"Establishing her new practice. That's what it is."

HE GOT A CALL from an unknown number in New York, but he didn't pick up and there wasn't any message. Then he got a call from Van Alsten's number.

It wasn't Van Alsten but Connie.

"They don't know exactly what went wrong," she said. A catch in her voice. A quaver. "They did the transplant. It seemed successful. All systems go, at least for me. But then he started crashing. His other kidney just, uh, stopped working. They said maybe the drinking had contributed. And then more . . . then some other organs. So now he's in a medically induced coma."

He felt the bottom drop out of his stomach.

His fondness for Van Alsten came home to him. Landed with weight.

He felt dull. Slow. Sapped of strength.

"Connie. I'm so sorry. I don't know what to say."

"I realize it's a lot to ask. But he doesn't have that many friends. Can you come see him? Please?"

"I'll come right away," he said.

Jason called while he was packing. His mother had been moved to the facility, he said. So he was going birding.

He would visit a wide, flat expanse of flooded desert called a playa, where tens of thousands of sandhill cranes were stopping on their migration.

Just before sunrise you could walk out and see the massive birds in their great numbers, before they took off.

Into the firmament.

Gil had always flown cheaply, seeing it as a moral obligation. He didn't fly enough for the miles that bumped you into first class. And the price of a seat there was obnoxious. More space for a few hours, plus mediocre booze and food. Who needed those minor amenities enough to pay a thousand extra bucks for them? His dollars were better spent on charity.

But the airlines had made it miserable in coach. He was a tall man and the tight spacing made his knees press into the seatback in front of him, annoying fellow travelers. When they chose to recline, it was a mild but lasting torment. He had to sit bolt upright for the duration, never relaxing.

Clouds of pretzel and cookie crumbs migrated to his sleeves and collar from the people eating next to him, and last time there'd been a raft of wet sneezes and coughs he felt himself inhaling.

Afterward, though he never got sick, he'd been sick for two weeks.

So this time he'd given in. He wasn't flying for leisure, was how he rationalized it. He was flying for an emergency. Plus first class had been the only seats left, on the flight he wanted. Now he sat in a bulkhead seat in first and was treated like one of the chosen.

Which he was. Chosen not on his merits but only by happenstance.

They said: Sir, can I get you anything? even while the rank and file were hustling down the aisle with their unwieldy luggage, pressed into each other's backs. They handed out heated, moist hand towels and warm nuts before takeoff. They pulled out the cloth curtain between compartments. Which served no purpose but to signal the class division.

From the other side, he'd looked at that curtain with a faint resentment.

He had to admit, though, the legroom was excellent.

But he wasn't able to savor it. The whole flight he was thinking about Van Alsten.

Or not thinking—he didn't know what to think. Only feeling. Heavy and flat.

What "medically induced coma" meant.

Whether they could induce him out of it again.

Whether they planned to try.

IN THE CAB to his hotel he looked out a window and saw the skyline come up. The bridges. His favorite part of the city. Maybe he'd walk over the Brooklyn, if he could get up early enough one morning to avoid the crowds. He used to run there at 6 a.m.

Fall was the best time in New York. He'd missed the color and smell of it, the turning of the seasons.

Somehow the city seemed more welcoming than it had when he left.

The stain of Lane's abandonment had faded.

"THANK YOU," SAID CONNIE. "Thank you so much for coming."

In the hospital waiting room visitors lounged on couches, some with their heads back, sleeping.

There were potted plants. Plastic. Vending machines and inspirational posters representing various faith traditions.

One of them he'd seen before, at a dentist's office: two sets of footprints making their way across the sand. All of a sudden, the two sets of footprints turned to one. And kept going.

How did the second set of footprints disappear? It was simple, the poster said. When the walking man became too tired and weak, the friend beside him lifted him onto his back. And carried him.

The name of the friend was Jesus.

"Is he doing . . . is he the same?"

"He'll always be the same," said Connie.

Her lips tried to smile.

So no, he thought. It was induced. But there would be no end to that inducement.

Van Alsten. And his performance.

Gil didn't want it to shut down. Felt, for a second, a jolt of desperation.

He clasped her hands and held them.

She'd gotten very thin, since Sky Harbor. Still recovering from her own surgery.

"His brother's with him now," she said. "I try to keep someone in there with him. So he's not alone. They say he doesn't know. But just in case."

"I see. Yes. That's good."

"I wanted to ask you. He still played his game twice a week. In Harlem. There's a number on his phone I think is his main contact for that. I'm just—I'm so tired of making calls. Would you mind doing it for me?"

"Of course not."

He'd met some of the guys Van Alsten played with but had never gone out with them.

She fished in her bag, which was sitting slumped on an end table, and brought out a cell. Van Alsten's.

"It's this one, I think. I'll go check on him."

The contact name was Legs. Part of Van Alsten's trash talk, maybe. He waited for Connie to disappear down the hall and then pushed the green button.

"Yo, Van," said the guy on the other end. "Where the fuck you been, man?"

"Actually, it's not him," said Gil. And explained.

Legs got agitated. He asked which hospital, but then dropped his phone. Gil had to tell him three times.

Next he called Vic.

"Oh, no," said Vic. "I had no idea."

Only two calls and he felt drained. No wonder Connie was tired of making them.

"You can go in now," she said, reappearing.

Beside her was Val Alsten.

No. His brother.

The spitting image, only slimmer and younger.

And wearing a well-cut suit. Likely bespoke.

There'd been the story about the private jet. Not the best one to recall just now, Gil chided himself as they shook hands.

The brother seemed to be in a trance. Glassy-eyed.

Connie pointed Gil down the hall.

THE PRIVATE ROOM was dimly lit. Van Alsten was hooked up to tubes and machines.

With his eyes closed he looked smaller. His slack face no longer imbued with personality. Even his large body under the sheet seemed barely there.

Gil sat down on the chair beside the bed.

"Hey," he said to the unmoving face. "It's Gil. I came to see you. You saved Connie's life, I hear. Well done."

He watched the face closely. Waiting.

Part of him had believed in a miraculous awakening.

LANE HAD NEVER reached out to him after she left. Never said a personal word. She sent only a message requesting he close their joint checking account "at his earliest convenience."

When he called her, which he only tried once, she'd blocked his number. It was true he could have tracked her down at work, could have shown up and made a scene, but he already felt humiliated.

It was her complete silence after the note *I met someone* that made it hard to assimilate her leaving. And the call blocking. As though he'd committed an offense so egregious that he deserved nothing.

And received it. In abundance.

HE ASKED CONNIE what he could do. She said maybe he could pick up some clothes, a shirt and pajama pants. Beneath the sheet Van Alsten was wearing a hospital gown.

"But *nobody* wants to be in a hospital gown," said Connie.

He heard, *Nobody wants to die in a hospital gown.*

Van Alsten had a favorite, worn-out T-shirt. His comfort shirt. A sentimental attachment.

How were the children? asked Gil.

They were both in college now, said Connie, brightening a little. The girl was at Columbia, the boy in England. The girl visited daily, and the boy was flying back tomorrow.

It was Thanksgiving week. He hadn't noticed.

She gave him a key and instructions and he left and took the subway. Their building had a large lobby with arches and old, art deco tilework on the floor—he'd met Van Alsten there once or twice, though he'd never gone up.

The doorman said how sorry he was. Van Alsten had always been good to him. He was a funny man, he said.

The front desk was bedecked with flowers.

"For him," said the doorman. "Mrs. V.A. said, keep them down here. She said, there's nobody up there to enjoy them. You tell her God bless."

All the way to the top, PH. Stepping out of the elevators, he was in a tranquil loft. Grays and blues. Understated and airy. On one wall of the foyer, a drawing that looked like a Vermeer.

Faint music was playing, the strains of a piano concerto. A stereo must have been left on. And a door to the terrace stood ajar.

It'd be a difficult place to rob, he guessed, unless you were a burglar trained in parkour.

Out on the terrace he could see the arch of Washington Square Park, right next door. The deck was a wraparound, so you could also look uptown. East and west. All the compass points.

Here were the roses Van Alsten had talked about, in wooden boxes. Many. Some were blooming.

He hadn't realized they could do that, in fall.

He found a hose and watered them, standing in the mist that carried onto his face and arms. From the rail he looked down at the tops of cars and pedestrians.

Then he made his way down a series of doors to the main bedroom. A Siamese cat was curled up sleeping on the bed. Opened its eyes when he came in. Stretched out all four legs lazily, then curled itself up again.

In the walk-in closet the T-shirt lay folded on the top of a neat pile: worn blue cotton with the number 12 and the words YALE UNIVERSITY.

HE'D TRIED HARD, after Lane left, to understand what he'd done to receive only silence. He couldn't recall ever raising his voice to her. Couldn't recall any callous acts. He'd been petty once or twice, he knew. Forgotten to replace the toilet paper roll.

But he'd given her all he had.

He'd seen her just one time. Maybe six months after she went.

He and Van Alsten had been at an overpriced restaurant in SoHo. It had French aspirations and a good bar. Van Alsten had got up to call Connie outside and left him at the bar nursing a martini. His grandmother's libation of choice.

Of all his grandmother's orderly habits, he recalled the evening martini most clearly. Her single indulgence. She'd measured it out, a ritual like clockwork at seven.

He drank one now and then. In remembrance.

He looked around the restaurant to pass the time, listened to the hum of conversation. He'd always liked being in restaurants.

And then he caught sight of a friend of Lane's, laughing at a table at the far end of the room. Deb was her name. He saw the back of a head across from her.

It had to be Lane. He knew the shape of the hair, the motion of her nodding.

His limbs acquired a bristling electricity. His legs shook on the barstool, his fingers trembled on the glass stem. The room turned kaleidoscopic. Louder and brighter. He couldn't move.

He felt locked into Lane's version of him. Disposable. Occupying a space, a slot in the world, for no good reason.

And therefore, in the end—after years of what he took to be closeness—not even worth a goodbye.

He must be less than no one. Because no one, at least, contained possibility.

Van Alsten came back in, sliding his cell phone into a jacket pocket. Saw right away that Gil was in an altered state.

Afterward Gil realized that was the instant he knew how perceptive Van Alsten could be. What a quick study.

He could read people well, when he decided to.

"It's that cheating bitch, isn't it," he said.

Gil had felt torn. He shouldn't let Van Alsten talk about her that way. But he couldn't speak.

"Sorry. Shouldn't say bitch," said Van Alsten, seeing it on his face. "That cheating *woman*. Just show me who she is."

Gil mustered enough strength to shake his head.

"I'm not going to beat her *up*, Gil," said Van Alsten. "I won't say anything to her. Scout's honor. Just like to have an image. Since I never met her. You know?"

He hadn't introduced them. He'd thought about it but had been fairly sure they wouldn't hit it off.

Two alphas. Both liked to hold forth. Capture a room's attention.

His shaking hand jolted his martini glass, which tipped and cracked at the rim, spilling liquid and olives onto the counter. A bartender wiped with a rag. Van Alsten slipped him a twenty and took Gil by the shoulders.

"Relax, man. Chill. Hey. Breathe. Take a deep breath. Now let it out slowly."

Once Gil calmed down enough to look toward the back of the restaurant again, Lane's table was empty. He swiveled toward the front windows and caught sight of her and Deb at the curb. Van Alsten followed his eyes.

Deb had an arm raised, hailing a cab.

Lane, in high heels and a long black coat, was looking down

into her bag, holding it open as she searched for something. She glanced up quickly.

"The one with the purse," said Van Alsten. "Right? It has to be."

A taxi pulled up and they got in.

VIC HAD ASKED to visit while Gil was there. With both of them in the room, maybe Connie could go get some dinner, Gil suggested. Take a break.

She had no appetite, she told him, but possibly she would go have a nap at her hotel. Just for an hour or so. She was staying nearby for convenience.

He'd watched her talking to a doctor. Saw the look on the doctor's face.

When Vic got to the hospital waiting room—his hair was grayer and his midsection thicker—Connie met him, shook his hand and held it, then left. The two of them went into the private room together.

Gil pulled a second chair up to the bed.

Vic sat for a minute, then extracted a velvet bag from his pocket. Inside were rosary beads that looked like pearls.

"Do you think it's OK?" he asked.

Van Alsten was a card-carrying WASP. And an atheist to boot.

But Gil could hear him say: Bring it. I don't give a fuck.

"I think he would appreciate the gesture," he translated.

Vic put the beads in one of Van Alsten's hands, draped them around the fingers.

"I'd like to say a prayer for him," said Vic.

Almighty and Everlasting God, preserver of souls, it went. We call upon Thee, O Lord, to grant Thy healing, that the soul of Thy servant, upon the hour of its departure from the body, may by the hands of Thy holy angels be presented . . .

The sun was setting as he prayed, graying head bowed and solid hands laced together. Gil averted his eyes. Trying to afford some privacy while still in the room.

On the white wall moved patterns of light and shade. Someone, maybe a child, had made bright-colored paper flowers. Origami. They stood in a jar on the windowsill, glued to the end of wooden chopsticks in a bouquet.

He would not pray, himself. But he wondered what else he could do for Van Alsten.

Or might have done. If he'd thought of it.

He imagined taking him to the desert. Standing beside him on the edge of the wide, flat playa Jason had talked about, watching thousands of cranes take off.

Van Alsten had never paid attention to wildlife—strictly an urban guy. Gil searched his memory for a single time he'd noticed a bird.

And was surprised to find one. They'd sat on a park bench together after one of the Harlem games. Van Alsten had been changing out of his shoes, because he never wore sneakers into bars. His personal dress code.

In bars much was permissible, to Van Alsten. But sneakers, never.

He pulled his pants on over his thin nylon shorts, while his gym bag rested on the cement at their feet.

A pigeon had strutted over to the bench. Angling for bread crumbs. Which they didn't have, of course.

Van Alsten had said: You know what he's thinking?

Gil said, I do *not* know. What the pigeon is thinking.

Van Alsten said, One day I'll fly up. Up, up, up, up.

And then I'm going to shit on you. And I will shit on all your friends.

HE SAT IN his hotel room, on the edge of the bed. At a loss. For some time, had no desire to move.

He wanted to say to someone: My friend is dying. And he isn't aware. He's dying without knowing it.

Was it better or worse not to know?

His parents hadn't known, or so his grandmother had assured him. Their death was sudden and without pain, she'd said to him when he was little.

Sudden and without pain, was what you said to children.

At least, in New England.

Without premeditation he reached for the room phone and dialed Lane's work number. He still knew it by heart. Near the end she'd stopped answering her cell for him during the day. Seeing the cyclist by then.

But she had a direct work line that didn't go through an assistant, and he'd taken to calling it when he had a question. Groceries. Or logistics.

Waiting as it rang, he thought: Likely she's left by now. It's been three years. She's probably changed jobs. Or married the cyclist. Moved to a small, quaint town up the Hudson.

Full of antique stores.

"Yes? What?" said her voice. Impatient.

Once he might have thought twice and hung up. But now he felt steady.

"Lane, hey. It's Gil."

Pause.

"Holy shit," she said slowly.

He found he couldn't say it after all. About Van Alsten.

"It's actually not a good time," she said. "People are here. In my office. But. You want to meet?"

HE GOT UP BEFORE DAWN and walked across the Brooklyn Bridge. Stood in the middle and looked down at the water. He would have welcomed an instant of wisdom.

However, none arrived. The water kept its own counsel.

WHEN HE GOT to the hospital Van Alsten's kids were there. The boy and the girl. Or rather, young man and young woman. Both slim and angular. Their faces puffy from crying.

Gil thought of Van Alsten in the Irish bar. Telling Vic, Kids are like furniture, but you can't sit on them. He'd edited his patter. Honing it for a new audience.

His children had been littler then.

Looking at them, he knew Van Alsten had been full of tenderness. But raw.

His words were his armor, that was all.

The hospital was running a couple more tests, said Connie.

But barring some unforeseen result, they were planning to take him off the machines tomorrow.

He wouldn't have wished to linger. He had a living will.

"I'm sure you need privacy," said Gil. "But is there anything I can do for you?"

"I *don't* need privacy. I'd like you to be in there with us. With him. If you can bear to. He'd want it. If he knew."

He was surprised.

"All right," he said. "Thank you. I'm—thank you. I'm honored."

HE'D CHOSEN the SoHo restaurant where he'd last seen her. With Van Alsten. The first restaurant name that came to him.

She looked older, he thought, approaching the table. Not a spiteful thought. An observation. Still beautiful. She would always be beautiful to him.

But her features seemed more brittle. At the corners of her eyes the wrinkles were less finely etched.

Those crow's-feet, visible when she laughed—so familiar.

"It's you," she said. She got up and embraced him. He found himself patting her back, then stopped. A reflex.

They sat.

"I heard you moved out West."

"I'm only back to visit a sick friend."

"I also heard you *walked* there. Really?"

"Yes. I did walk."

She shook her head.

"Well," she said. "At least you finally *did* something."

She had a way of insulting him with a half-smile on her face. That way the insult was blunted. At the beginning he'd assumed she was joking. Over time, not so much.

He thought, I never took money for it, true. But I always did something. At least, I always worked. Just like you.

He didn't say it. She measured success by career, the way most people did. And it was fair and accurate to say he'd never had one. He'd offered up his time, done what others needed him to do.

They could put it on his gravestone: *He tried to be of use.*

She didn't ask about his sick friend, and he found himself thinking: She doesn't *deserve* to know.

As though the knowledge would be a gift to her. Instead of a small burden. Of having to express sympathy.

He didn't want to hear that dutiful expression.

A waiter asked if they wanted lunch. Just coffee, thanks, Gil said.

His impulse was to order a beer, to remove him and buoy him up, but he didn't want its benefits, for once. The warmth, the generosity.

He wanted to see coldly. Be lucid.

Lane ordered an herbal tea.

She said she'd had job offers, but none lucrative enough to lure her away from her current position. She was editor-in-chief now, but it had gotten boring, she told him.

She talked about some women they both knew. One struggled with Lyme disease. Another with a colicky baby.

"Listen," she said. "I know I dealt with it poorly. Back then."

"You mean. By sleeping with the Tour de France guy?"

He didn't say it angrily. He wanted to understand.

She shrugged. "I couldn't have left without that. And I had to. It's more like, I should have been in touch."

He felt a prick of hostility. At the understatement.

Then a wave of something duller and softer. He wasn't sure what. Indifference?

"Well. Yes. That would have helped me," he said. "At the time."

"It didn't work out. With him."

"Oh no?"

"Yeah. No. It didn't last."

Was he supposed to say he was sorry?

"It lasted for a while," she said. "With you and me."

"A very long time, I'd say. Considering."

She sipped her tea, put the cup down again.

"Considering?"

He hesitated.

It had been clear and forthright, when it existed only in his mind. Said aloud in this surface exchange, it would seem melodramatic. No doubt.

Very simple things could come out sounding that way.

"Considering that you always said you loved me. When I said it to you. The ritual—I love you and I love you too. But in fact you didn't. You only stayed with me for so long out of habit. And because I had money."

She studied him warily. As though he was trying to make her give up a small, valuable object.

Then seemed to yield.

"I think," she said, "maybe. The first six months?"

She slumped in her chair. As though she'd just realized how exhausting it had been to sit up straight that whole time.

Cupped both of her hands around the teacup. Blew a ripple across the liquid's surface.

And let her unfocused gaze settle on something below his face. It had been difficult for her to admit.

"Then, OK. A question. If I may."

"Sure."

"When we first met. That night at the pool hall. Did you already know? That I had money?"

She squinted at him slightly, as though his face was casting an unwelcome light. Shifted her angle in her seat.

"Well. Not how much. But I knew who those guys worked for. I mean, of course I knew *that*. They were my friends, sort of. And someone had said you were a client."

So his question was answered. After so long.

He'd attached everything to her once. Everything that he was. And wasn't.

But he'd been mistaken. The error had always been his.

He sat there and felt the last atoms of attachment fall away.

BEFORE THEY PARTED on the sidewalk, she moved to hug him. He felt an aversion to her touch he hadn't felt only an hour before. Stood in place as she applied a light pressure. And then turned and walked away from her.

Had a sense of the restaurant behind him, the shape of his

last two visits there. Lane standing outside it. The time with Van Alsten, when her ghosting of him had seemed like such a clear verdict. Her judgment the judgment of all.

This time, the clarity of his own verdict. As basic as his question: he'd misplaced his trust. Willfully blind.

Both of her decisions, to stay and then to go, had been purely about herself.

Her absence had not made him no one. Just as her presence had not made him someone.

In all of her choices he'd been more like anyone. They'd had little to do with him.

Maybe he hadn't exactly failed, back then. Only failed to see. And hoped—a hope that ended in disappointment.

He had a strong feeling they would never meet again.

AT THE APPOINTED HOUR he went into Van Alsten's room with the family and stood at the foot of the bed.

Connie and the children and brother clustered on either side. Medical personnel filed through the door, including the doctor who'd kept shaking his head.

Van Alsten wore his favorite T-shirt. They'd left the rosary beads draped over his fingers.

They were a tribute, Connie said.

She'd shown him a card Vic had sent. *For all that he has given*, Vic had written, *he will rest in eternal peace.*

The doctor asked if any of them wanted to say anything, but they murmured no, they'd already said it.

The daughter went in for one last kiss to her father's cheek. Then stood back, crying, as Connie put an arm around her.

All the staff did was flick switches and push buttons. Machines beeped. Machines stopped beeping.

Van Alsten looked as he had before.

As he had before, except that now he had departed.

GIL FELT HE NEEDED a dose of strong liquor, after the goodbyes were said.

He knew what he would do. He'd never been more certain.

He would call up his old friend.

He would call up Van Alsten, and they would go have a drink.

VULTURE

TOM CAME OVER crowing the news: his mother had done it! She did it! She was great!

Gil agreed, she *was* great. But how, in this case?

She had talked to the homeowners' association. It had changed the rules. "Youth" were allowed to skateboard in cul-de-sacs now. If they were supervised.

"For real?" said Gil.

"I swear!"

"Strong. Very strong."

"I'm sorry about your friend," said Tom, sobering. "My dad told me. He said he wasn't even old. And that he was just trying to help someone. It's really sad."

"Well," said Gil. "Yes. Thank you."

It touched him. A small boy's condolences.

He said he'd like to see Tom's neck.

"Oh. It's all good." Tom bent forward, obliging.

The punctures had healed.

"And nothing else happened? He's leaving you alone?"

"He doesn't *take* the bus anymore," said Tom. "He gets driven."

You could do so much with so little. At times.

Other times, with all the privilege there was, nothing.

"YOU KNOW WHAT HAPPENED, RIGHT?" asked Ted.

They stood in the backyard at sunset beside Tom's punching bag. Set their whiskeys down on a wide, flat tree branch. A convenient surface. Took turns kicking the bag, Ted with some energy, Gil idly.

"No. Please tell me."

"The man who runs the neighborhood association is this total old lech. He came to that housewarming thing. The guy with the tacky, offensive Hawaiian shirt? It had big red flowers printed on it and native women in grass skirts?"

"Oh yeah," said Gil, nodding slowly. The shirt was memorable. "And sandals?"

"He's a developer, I heard. Casinos in Vegas. I did some quick research—off-Strip. Ridiculously leveraged. He hung around Ardis while she was fixing drinks. He *fully* looked down her dress. I was there."

"And saw—what? A bra?"

"There *was* no bra. One of those dresses you can't wear them with. He clearly, obviously leaned."

"He *leaned*? A lean is wrong."

"Sarah saw too. She'll testify to it."

"So you're saying that Ardis had sway with him. Because of . . ."

"Tits," said Ted. "Tit view. Saw tits."

"Would he actually be influenced by that? One minor breast sighting? In regard to the weighty matter of the bylaw on youth skateboarding?"

"Come on now, Gil. Are you familiar with your fellow man?"

"No. Not really."

"Then let me enlighten you. Yes, is the answer. Yes."

"Well. OK then. Put to good use, I guess. Your wife's, uh . . ."

"Ti—uh, breasts."

"As you say."

"We won't speak of them again."

"I don't plan to."

Gil got tired of kicking the bag and stopped. He wished there were fireflies. He hadn't seen any here.

"I miss the monsoon season," he said. "The wildlife."

"Those toads that come out around a storm," agreed Ted. Delivered one last kick. "The big, fat ones."

"You can lick them, I heard."

"If you want to have mystical visions."

"Hallucinations. But then you writhe in agony. Poisonous secretions on the skin."

"I was never a toad-licker. Even in college."

"You never licked a toad?"

"You're gonna tell me you *did*?"

"No way. I never licked a toad either."

"We missed the toad-licking boat."

"We went to school back East. A shortage of desert toads. That was *our* problem."

"Oh. There's a light on in the dining room," said Ted. "Ardis is home."

"I'll leave you to it, then."

"No, hey. Come in. For a nightcap. She'll be glad to see you."

"You sure?"

"She always is. An extrovert. My cross to bear."

"I won't mention the lecherous guy. Leaning."

"Make sure you don't. She thinks it was her appeal to reason. She thinks that's what carried the day."

"Innocent?"

"Feminist."

"Hey, I get it. I'm a feminist too."

"As well you should be."

They headed inside carrying their whiskeys.

SINCE THE HOTTEST WEATHER had passed, he started walking. After he got up but before his first cup of coffee. He slipped through the hole in the back fence and turned to his right up the wash until it got too rocky and brushy, then turned back and walked the other way. There the land got wide and rolling, and you could go for a mile.

One morning he was startled by the upflight of a large black bird. Red head. Wattle.

A turkey vulture. Like the ones he'd seen on the long walk.

People looked down on them, as carrion-eaters. But they were the peaceable recyclers of the dead.

He'd disrupted its meal.

He stepped closer and saw what was left of a quail. Its black plume gave it away. A brown-and-black face mask, so it was male.

It must be quail-hunting season. He would check.

He scrounged around for a stick and flipped it over. There was shot in one wing. But not in the breast or head.

Someone had left it there without making a kill shot. It might have suffered for some time.

It looked so neat.

Still beautiful, despite being dead.

ON THE LONG WALK HE'D SEEN so much roadkill. Lying on the asphalt shoulders. Mostly birds and coyotes.

It had struck him, passing their still forms, how peaceful they looked lying there.

Sometimes there had been carnage: flesh tossed and ripped by tires. Leaving a debris field of blood and feathers or fur, torn tendons or broken bones. In those bodies, the illusion of peace could not be sustained.

He'd had to look away, wincing, until the scene was behind him.

But most of them lay on the roads as if in state. Resting after a struggle. Having relinquished the fight.

He'd thought of how he would look—how any person would, in a similar position. Not peaceful or beautiful at all.

He'd been puzzled by it. The surrender that seemed to reside in the animals' dead bodies.

And the sadness that settled on him as he walked away from them.

HE'D ONLY BEEN GONE for a week, but when he went back to the shelter both Lori and Mari had moved on.

Mari had relocated to California. But Lori was back with her husband. And her dog.

He was in treatment, said the shelter's director.

Not the dog. The husband, she clarified.

He had a trip to the grocery store on his schedule and then an animated movie at a mall multiplex with a mother and two children. The woman in denim.

The director told him she didn't want to be at the shelter. Her presence was the result of a family intervention. She'd complied grudgingly.

Ricki, said the woman. Short for Patricia. She never went by Patty or Pat. Didn't answer to them.

He had no plans to call her Patty or Pat. So OK, good, he said.

The children—twin boys with mullets and side rattails they called Padawan braids—didn't seem to like him much either. When he tried smiling at them, they scowled.

SARAH TEXTED. She was so sorry about Van Alsten.

He wrote back to thank her.

After a few more days she texted, *Ardis says you're not up for dating, or whatever. I get it. You want to get together sometime anyway? Just friends. I work long hours. I never meet anyone I like outside work.*

He'd been so tense about her. But he was freer of Lane now.

When she haunted him, it wasn't out of longing but regret. Regret over his own unwillingness to face the facts, back then. These days, when he thought of her, instead of falling into misery he only kicked himself.

Preferable.

He still worried about the intersections. Without Van Alsten, all he had was the family of four. And far off, vaguely, Vic.

But just friends, she had said.

So he wrote back, *Sure. What do friends do?*

And she replied: *Huh. I don't know. Mine only go drinking. Pick a number. 1. Party? 2. Hike? 3. Mini-golf?*

He wrote back *Drinking.*

That wasn't a number.

I know.

HE WAS PROTECTIVE. Of Tom, yes, but also Ted and Ardis. Even Clem. Though he had little to offer her, at this time in their lives. An occasional minor service was all she wanted from him.

And his pinball machines. Clem came over to play on them when she had nothing better to do, even let Tom come with her. As long as he played a machine that wasn't right next to hers, she warned him. She couldn't stand it when he hovered at her elbow.

Tom hung *around* so much. That was the worst thing about little brothers: their habit of being there.

He might have had the woman Ellen for a next-door neighbor. Or the casino builder. He didn't deserve what he had been given.

He never had.

But he accepted it.

HE FOUND MORE QUAIL in the wash. Three, four, five. Saw one being carried off by a stray dog, a feathery bundle in its mouth.

They'd been shot, like the first. He guessed it was all right that other animals were getting the benefit of the birds' bodies, but it also pissed him off.

It was one thing to hunt, then eat what you killed. Another to use the birds for target practice.

Jason said barely anyone ate wild-caught Gambel's quail. Many game hunters preferred private preserves, where they could pay for canned hunts.

In these preserves doves and pheasants were raised to be hunted, then flushed out for the clients as they pulled their triggers. Some of them constantly: fingers got tired. Muscle cramping occurred. Automatic counters tallied the kills on a leaderboard.

Jason had a cousin who went on game safaris down to South America. Shot thousands of birds on a single trip.

His girlfriend posted the count on social media. With emojis of clapping hands and smiley faces.

HE COULDN'T GET UP EARLY enough to surprise the hunter. Just never saw him—only the aftermath.

And never heard shots, either.

Still more puzzling. Silencers, Jason told him, weren't really a thing. Outside movies and maybe organized crime.

He looked up night hunting. "Nocturnal hunting is becoming more popular all the time," advised a website.

But birds were not preferred nocturnal targets, the website said. Because, with exceptions like owls, they slept at night.

Or moved far above, out of sight in the sky, in their great migrations.

On the other hand, raccoons, ringtails, foxes, bobcats, and javelinas were good animals to kill at night. An added bonus was, they let their guard down. In the dark.

Even so, he went to another site that sold night-hunting gear. And ordered the most expensive night-vision goggles he could find.

SARAH TEXTED THAT ARDIS was coming with them for the drinks. She'd been working hard and needed to blow off steam. Ted was away for a couple of days, but Clem could babysit.

Good, thought Gil—even less of a date. He'd be one of the girls.

It was a brewpub downtown, woody and high-ceilinged with exposed ductwork. It sold only wine and regional microbrews, and the hipster bartender talked about beer as though it was high art.

Gil asked what they had that was closest to a Pabst Blue Ribbon. Sarah gave a light trill of laughter.

The bartender ignored the laugh and answered with polite condescension. He pitied Gil, that was obvious, but had to be faithful to his patrons' tastes. It was his sovereign duty.

Ardis sampled Gil's beer once it came.

"It doesn't taste anything *like* PBR," she said.

"He failed you," said Sarah.

"Disgusting," said Gil, when the bartender was out of earshot. "Like drinking bongwater."

It tasted good, of course.

Sarah told them about her ex-husband's obsession with craft beer. It had gotten on her nerves. It was like being a wine connoisseur, but supposedly more manly. Because it had a DIY component. He'd tried to brew some once, and bought himself an expensive homebrew kit, but ended up with rotten soup in a bucket.

She and Ardis relived college a bit: there was a group of girls in the corner with Greek letters on their pink hoodies. Sarah said *she* should have joined a sorority, at least she'd have had a social life. She'd barely left her dorm room, she was hitting the books so hard. Organic Chem had kicked her ass.

Ardis said she might have been a LUG, if she'd joined a sorority. She'd known some girls from a Christian one, where premarital sex was against the rules, who figured out a whole lesbian work-around.

They'd had more sex than anyone she knew, she said. Just not with men.

She regretted how boring and heterosexual her dating life had been. And now it was too late.

LUG? asked Gil.

Lesbian Until Graduation, Sarah told him.

They were surprised. How could he not know that?

"There's a lot I don't know," said Gil. "Sheltered. You shouldn't be surprised."

He asked how the two of them knew each other.

"Met at a conference in Dallas," said Ardis. "I was on a panel."

"'The Psychotherapeutics of Dying,'" said Sarah.

"Yes! Sarah was slumming, coming into a room full of shrinks. Some of them didn't even have doctorates! Like me. I have a lowly master's."

"What can I say," said Sarah. "I needed a break from real medicine. Plus *Dying* was in the title. I figured it might be relevant to my surgeries."

They both laughed.

"Bad joke. Sorry. But honestly," said Sarah, "she was a breath of fresh air. You were! Those blowhards up on the stage with you? You refused to use their jargon. Said everything plainly. You were articulate. And it didn't hurt that you looked like a supermodel. In a crowd of stodgy middle-aged men. I was drawn to you."

"She came up to me afterward and we cut the rest of the panels and went to a diner. When Ted got his relocation offer, I thought, Phoenix! That's where Sarah is."

"I got matched here. For my residency. And just stayed," said Sarah. "What about you, Gil? You lived in New York before, right? How'd you end up here?"

"I had a bad breakup. I needed a change."

"So you randomly picked Phoenix, Arizona? Just packed up a moving truck and drove across the country?"

"Actually I walked here."

"Ha ha," said Ardis.

"No but I did, I walked."

They gaped at him.

"*Stop*," said Ardis. "Are you being serious right now?"

"You *walked*," said Sarah. "From New York to *Phoenix*?"

"Twenty-fourth Street and Madison. Where my apartment was. To my new house. Here."

"What is that—like, three thousand miles?" asked Ardis.

"Two thousand five hundred. Approximately. It took me almost five months."

"How have I known you this whole time and that never came up?" asked Ardis.

He shrugged. "It's not much of a story. It was mostly big roads. Interstates, even. Because to go by the small roads would have taken a lot longer. It went like this: the same, the same, the same. Then, for a few miles, slightly different. The same, the same, the same, the same . . . then slightly different. I met some truckers. And saw a lot more roadkill than I ever wanted to."

Sarah was studying him.

"Gil. I don't mean to pry. But why did you *walk* across the whole country?"

He thought of Lane at the restaurant. *You finally* did *something.*

"I guess . . . partly to see if I could."

They sat there holding their drinks, still gazing at him with curiosity.

"But also, I wanted to pay for something. When you have a lot of money, you never pay for *anything*. You never feel the cost, so you live like everything is free. There's never a trade-off. Never a choice or a sacrifice, unless you give up your time. I wanted the change to cost me. You know? I wanted to earn it."

They were quiet for a minute.

"So did it work?" asked Sarah. "Did you earn the marvel of living in this great city of Phoenix?"

A good question. He considered it.

"I'm not sure," he said finally. "I just walked. For a fucking long time."

They laughed again. Him too.

Sarah said this outing was her last gasp of freedom for a while: her sister was flying in from Houston for the holidays with her family, which included three children—a baby, a toddler, and a preschooler. They would be staying in her house. For two weeks beginning the first night of Chanukah.

They would have to do the rituals. Her sister was observant.

"My house is small," she told Gil. "Not like you guys'. I downsized when I got divorced. One kid is potty training. It'll be ugly."

"Who stays for two weeks?" asked Ardis. "Six upper-middle-class Americans in a one-bedroom bungalow! Cruel and unusual punishment."

"My sister likes to economize."

Ardis turned to Gil. "You *never* talk about your family," she said.

An awkward juncture. He didn't want to be a downer. An honest answer would derail the conversation.

"You don't want to know," he said.

"What," said Sarah. "Are they Trump supporters?"

"Fundamentalists?" asked Ardis. "QAnon? Cultists?"

"Nothing like that," he said. "Just dead."

"Oh," said Ardis.

"Oh," said Sarah. "Oh, I'm so sorry."

"Happened a long time ago. And it was a small family."

Neither could jump in to save it. Trying to find the right expressions of sympathy.

"My mother and father died when I was little. Car crash. I lived with my grandmother till I was about Tom's age. In Boston. But then she died too. There wasn't anyone else. My grandfather had been in the Air Force, KIA in Korea, and she never remarried. The other set of grandparents wasn't around because my mother had been a foundling. That was what my grandmother called it. Left on the doorstep of an orphanage. I never went into foster care. My grandfather's family were oil and gas barons. Despoiled the earth and made a lot of money. So after my grandmother died I had appointed guardians. They rotated through their duties. Like a relay team. Responsible but distant. Just, kind of, meeting the basic needs. In the house that she'd left me. I was like a fly trapped in amber. Eventually I turned eighteen and went to college. Then I moved to New York. Then here. That's my biography. I don't remember my parents."

Ardis lifted her wineglass.

"Let's drink to them," she said.

SARAH CALLED UP a ride on an app afterward, embracing them both before she got in, and Ardis asked if he was driving and would take her home. She'd left her own car at work. She'd only had two glasses of wine but said she felt buzzed.

Hadn't had much food today, she confessed. No time between sessions. Didn't eat in her office, because the smell of her meal could linger and distract a client. She used to have lunch at her desk on busy days, she told him, until the time when a patient with suicidal ideation smelled garlic and went on for fifty minutes about his mother's pesto.

Gil had drunk two beers, but it had been mitigated by a pretentious bundle of truffle-oil French fries. To convince her of his fitness to drive, he hopped for twenty steps and performed a routine that featured touching his thumb to his nose and walking backward.

"You *seem* drunk," scolded Ardis. "Only a drunk man would feel OK looking so asinine."

"How dare you," he said, but they were both grinning.

AFTER THE NIGHT-VISION goggles arrived it took him a while to get a handle on their technical aspects. They were binoculars you strapped to your head. He put them on and stood in front of the mirror. Looked like a cyborg: half man and half machine.

He bought protective sheaths for his calves, also—gaiters, they were called. Stalking around in the wash, with his focus on the optics, he'd need protection from cacti.

And possibly from rattlesnakes, though they were underground this time of year.

Then he decided he also needed a jacket with padding.

At a certain point he realized he might be procrastinating.

HE GOT A BIZARRE CALL from his lawyer, who was on his money manager's staff.

A man had contacted him. A man in his sixties who went by "Dag." Dag had done considerable research to track down the lawyer and had emailed a request. The lawyer was reluctant to convey it, but in the end was bound.

When the man was young, he had driven impaired, the lawyer said. He was the one who'd hit Gil's parents.

He'd gone to prison for it and eventually been released. But now he wished to speak to Gil, the lawyer said.

His grandmother had never told him the man's name. It was a matter of public record, but he'd never looked it up. Hadn't wanted to know.

What would it give him now to hear the man speak?

He certainly didn't have to, the lawyer said.

The lawyer wouldn't, in his position. Personally. Hell no.

JASON HAD DOWNLOADED a dating app. Posted a picture and a self-description. He showed them to Gil.

But so far, no takers.

Man of birds, said his profile.

THE NEIGHBORHOOD association had a website. Discussions of road-sign improvements, speed bumps, fire-engine response times. Competing pictures of well-tended gardens.

"Click on the Nitty Gritty link," said Ardis, leaning over his shoulder at the computer. "That's where the dirt is."

It was a forum for complaints. Residents could post by name or anonymously, and the association would follow up.

Three mailboxes in a row had been bashed in. Had it been captured on anyone's security camera?

A beater truck was spotted, parked suspiciously. It had wrinkling paint on the hood. And a colorful Virgin of Guadalupe hanging from the rearview mirror.

"What does that mean?" asked Gil. "How do you park suspiciously?"

"You just drive an old truck," said Ardis.

"And then you park," he agreed.

"Poor people in the hood. Call out the National Guard!"

She came from a working-class family.

One homeowner kept finding cigarette butts in the soil of his ornamental cabbage containers. Had never caught the offender. It was like having a poltergeist, he wrote.

"A smoking poltergeist," said Gil.

"The most dangerous kind," agreed Ardis. "A ghost with no respect for its body."

Rap music with a powerful bass was heard late at night coming from a particular house. But the homeowners wouldn't even cop to liking hip-hop! Were they secret Airbnb-ers?

One hundred percent against the bylaws, someone wrote angrily.

An unknown individual had posted signs on telephone poles advertising the sale of Girl Scout cookies. With a phone number.

Posting signs for commercial purposes was forbidden.

"That Girl Scout phone is probably a burner," said Gil.

Someone's dog was a serial urinator on the rear tire of a Mercedes. S-Class.

Another dog, or possibly the same offender, was dropping stealth bombs on pristine lawns.

The owner left them there. Using his dog as a weapon.

CALLING FROM NEXT DOOR, Sarah asked to come over. Needed a break from her family. She'd wanted a place to hide for an hour or two, and Ardis and Ted had turned out to be busy.

Gil fixed her a drink at the bar.

Then Jason showed up, unannounced.

He told them he was frustrated by the lack of interest in him. On the dating app.

Sarah asked to see what he'd put up.

"So, do you want a little feedback?" she asked.

"I don't know?" said Jason.

"Let me put it another way. Do you want dates?"

More than zero would be good, he conceded.

"Well, I wouldn't lead with the birdwatching," she said.

"But I don't *want* to go out with a lady who's not a birder," said Jason. "What would we even *do*?"

"You think you don't. But what if you could introduce her? To the pleasures of birding?"

Jason cocked his head. "Huh."

"Right? There's a whole universe of birds out there, and you could introduce her to it!"

"What if she doesn't even like the Migratory Bird Treaty Act?"

"Win her over."

"WHY DON'T YOU POST about the quail?" suggested Ardis, during their cocktail hour before a Sunday dinner at his place. He was in his bartender role. "You know. On the neighborhood website?"

Gil considered it, then shook his head.

"I mean, it *is* quail-hunting season," he told them. "Till February. It's only illegal if I can prove it's happening at night. In daytime, it's fully legal. On state land. I need the element of surprise."

"Show us your gear," urged Ardis.

"Really?"

"Absolutely," said Ted. "We want to see you in citizen's arrest mode."

He slipped out from behind the bar and went to his bedroom. Kitted himself out. Including the goggles.

Looked black and bulky, like a guy on a SWAT team.

Then he crept back into the bar area, up behind them. Crouched down in a stealth pose, camera in hand. Coughed theatrically.

When they pivoted, snapped a picture of their faces.

"Wow, shit," said Ted. "Clothes make the man, I guess. I'm actually intimidated."

"I have a newfound respect for you," said Ardis.

CHRISTMAS CAME AND WENT. Gil spent it next door. Clem got a new phone, and Tom got a half-pipe in the backyard.

By New Year's Eve Sarah's family had left. Her two-year-old nephew had toilet-trained in the living room, she told them. He had sat on his travel potty as if on a throne, calmly surveying sofas and family members and mealtimes. He watched videos on a tablet as he deliberated.

Mostly they were videos of soft-voiced women, slowly unboxing toys from plastic packaging.

She threw a party to celebrate her liberation. It was teeming with other surgeons and their families. The surgeons drank like fishes. Gil had never seen people who drank so hard. Not since a certain party he remembered from senior year, anyway.

A roommate had dragged him to it. On that occasion, after a beer-bong incident, a frat boy had been taken to the hospital with alcohol poisoning. His nickname was Boner.

They watched the ball drop on TV. Not midnight yet, out West, but no one seemed to care. The kids threw confetti everywhere. Tom was jubilant.

"That'll be hell to vacuum," Gil said to Sarah.

Later she wanted them to sleep together, and he did too.

He'd forgotten what it felt like to be wanted.

Had known once, long ago. Though only for six months, as it turned out.

It felt like being alive. Only more.

RAVENS

DAG, WHO'D KILLED GIL'S parents, didn't have the resources
to travel but had asked for a face-to-face.

"He wants to do a *video call* with you?" asked Ted.

Gil nodded.

"Why video?" said Ardis.

"More personal, he said."

"That guy's got balls of steel," said Ted.

HIS FIRST NIGHT EXPEDITION was fruitless, along with
his second. He walked along the wash fiddling with his goggles.
Avoiding cactus. Once saw the hind quarters of a coyote as it
slunk off behind a shrub. Its bushy tail.

Once he saw a great-horned owl in flight.

After an hour or two, he got tired and went back to bed. Sarah called them sorties.

"What are you going to do?" she asked. "If you find a guy with a gun creeping around out there? He'll have the night-vision gear too, won't he? And if your suspicions are right, he's an old hand at it. Presumably. You're just a rookie. Maybe he'll see you first."

"I'll hunker down," he said. "Hide. Try to get a picture. But even if I can't, I'll follow him. See which house he goes back into. Then, later, we can have a civil conversation."

"Huh, a covert action. I hope you don't get shot."

JASON HAD HAD THREE different dates with different ladies—he always said "ladies"—but none of them had accepted his invitations to go out looking for birds.

The dates had not ended well.

"LISTEN. If I do that video call," he asked Sarah, "would you mind being there with me?"

Maybe the man needed to acknowledge the past. Maybe the space for a small reckoning was easy to give.

"I mean," she said. "I mean, I'm not sure why you'd agree to talk to him."

"Just in case."

"In case what?"

"In case it's important. To him. Not me."

"I'm not in favor," said Sarah. "But if you feel you have to, I'll be there."

He was happier when she was there. In general. And in specific.

Sometimes he was incredulous. That she wanted to be.

But she convinced him.

ARDIS KEPT SAYING he needed to throw a party, too. Follow up on her housewarming. Neighbors didn't talk anymore. They could be the great uniters. In free food was solidarity.

Seriously. It would help build community, she claimed.

For parties, castles were better than houses of glass, she said. Hidden nooks and crannies as well as large rooms. Dark corners, secret alcoves.

He didn't have to do much himself, she urged. He could call an event planner, if he liked.

Sarah offered to help.

At first he resisted.

AFTER A MINUTE OF FUTZING with the interface, he saw the call coming in and clicked the answer button. Behind him Sarah leaned against a chair, drinking coffee.

Dag was a nondescript older man, pale with patchy red skin on his face. Gaps where teeth were missing. He'd done some hard living.

He coughed, thanked Gil for taking his call. He wanted to say, he still thought of Gil's parents. Though forty years had passed.

He'd thought of Gil too, when he was inside. Had Gil gotten his letters, back when he was a kid?

No, said Gil. No letters.

Even if a prison letter had reached his grandmother, she'd never have given it to him. Or even opened it. It would have been tossed into the trash without a second thought.

Dag suffered from lupus, among other illnesses. He lived in what Gil guessed was a halfway house—a men's home, he called it. He was using a shared computer. It had been hard to find steady work, after he got out. He'd fallen victim to opioid addiction.

It was an epidemic.

"Yes," said Gil. "I know. I'm sorry to hear that."

But he'd gotten clean and now was seven months sober. *Sober as a judge*, he said.

"Has to be hard," said Gil.

"Shit! *I* know what this is," whispered Sarah. "He's going to ask you for money."

Gil shook his head, disbelieving.

Dag said his men's home was in the Baltimore area. The shared bathroom had cockroaches. Size of your thumb, he said. The shared kitchen had no working oven. He had to buy food at a gas station mini-mart, because he couldn't drive and there were no grocery stores nearby.

The mini-marts sold microwavable burritos, though. And hot dogs.

Luckily, said Dag, he had a friend in Jesus Christ.

"Ah. Yes, a friend," said Gil.

He thought of the footprints in the sand.

"But Jesus was always short on cash," whispered Sarah.

Dag said he was trying every day. But the system was locked down against people like him. Doors were barred. Like prison. Even once you were out, you were in.

Gil wouldn't know how that was. Still, yeah, if there was anything he could do to help . . . Dag had been praying on it.

"But what *can* I do?" Gil asked the guy.

He didn't want to admit she'd been right.

"Just if there's anything you can spare, man. You know. Just anything you can spare."

"*There* it is," said Sarah.

POSSIBLY HE WAS FIXATED on apologies. Always expecting people to apologize to you, then feeling slighted when they didn't: Was that a telltale sign of some dire pathology? Narcissistic personality disorder? A persecution complex?

He would ask Ardis.

Or maybe they did apologize, but the apology didn't meet your high standards. For instance, Dag had said he thought of Gil's parents. He'd said he wrote letters. And maybe he had. Maybe that served. Maybe he'd said everything in the letters, and there was nothing more he could say.

He lay awake thinking of Dag's request. Sure, it was out of line. So brash it was insulting. No man who'd killed another guy's parents while driving drunk should then feel justified in asking him for their legacy.

However, Gil *had* that legacy. He didn't. And it was logical to ask. If you didn't care about justification.

You can't help everyone, said Sarah. Philanthropy 101. Why

would you choose *him* to help? There were plenty of people out there who needed it. People who'd never killed anyone.

Gil told her how once, when he was straight out of college, he'd decided to give up his grandparents' ill-gotten wealth. And fend for himself.

For several weeks after he made this decision, he'd felt euphoric. So excited he could barely contain it. As though he was standing on the edge of a great abyss, not dark but filled with light. Towering cliffs and a sparkling river.

Like the Grand Canyon, maybe. Although he'd never seen it.

A realm of possibility—his life was no longer set. His life could be anything.

Everywhere he went, everything he did during those few weeks was colored vibrantly. He listened to inspiring music, full of extra energy every morning when he woke up. He broke into a run on sidewalks, only realizing as he slowed down that he was grinning crazily.

He'd told Hadley of his revelation at a rare in-person meeting.

Saying it, though, he found he couldn't do it justice.

Couldn't explain to Hadley, in his oak-and-leather office with its fine appointments and wide views of the Manhattan skyline, how heavy the money was. A coat of shame he always had to wear.

Or how the thought of not having it anymore was like discovering he could fly.

Most people, Hadley said, felt just the opposite. For the reality was, it was money that set you free. Not the lack of it. Gil couldn't know this yet because he'd always had money. But the second he didn't, he would see.

Actually, Gil wanted to say, he hadn't always had money. At

least, that he knew of. In his grandmother's gray house they'd lived simply, as she had always lived. Austerely, even. You had to finish every morsel, at supper, to be in the "clean plate club." And there was never dessert.

Except, on rare occasions, baked apples with cinnamon. Her specialty.

He had five outfits, one for each day of school, which he washed and dried himself on the weekends. The clothes—serge trousers with darts at the waist and button-down shirts—were nothing like what the other kids wore.

In grade school he'd been a pariah. Mostly because of those clothes.

He also laundered his two sets of what she called "play togs"—weirdly shaped flared corduroys and wool sweaters—and her own garments. He remembered them perfectly: large, square underwear, tan stockings, and tweed skirts. She taught him how to fold and iron, but her arthritis prevented her from directly assisting.

At Christmas there was a stocking full of walnuts in shells he had to crack and thick-skinned oranges that were hard to peel. Then dry inside and full of seeds. Under the tree were a pair of new shoes or boots she'd chosen and two or three educational books. They were on subjects like orienteering or how to make a fire with sticks.

Once a board game: Parcheesi.

After she died, he'd lived in much the same way with the guardians. Except that his clothes got more normal, since he was permitted to pick them out himself on supervised shopping trips. Which improved his social standing.

Each Christmas, in his teenage years, he received a gift certificate and a stocking purchased, premade, from a candy company.

It was only when he turned eighteen that the trustees had told him about the money. In the meeting, at first, he'd thought it was fantastic news. At Christmas, he could buy himself anything he wanted from then on.

Never again a thick-skinned orange. Never again walnuts. Or a net-bag stocking sealed in a factory.

But soon enough the heaviness came on.

Hadley didn't know how it had been. And Gil couldn't tell him. He listened patiently, nodding, as Gil explained earnestly that anyway, on a moral level, all very rich people should give away their wealth.

First, the ones who hadn't earned it. Next, the ones who just had way too much.

At this Hadley winced. Visibly.

But if Gil was honest, that wasn't his reason.

His reason was himself. The prospect of feeling free.

Hadley told Gil he understood, and if this was Gil's final decision, he was willing to liquidate the assets. He was there only to fulfill Gil's wishes. And offer professional guidance.

Only a single thing would he ask: Take a year to think it over. A whole year. He had to ask this, in honor of Gil's grandmother. She would have insisted.

You're very young, Hadley said kindly. Condescending, but meaning to be kind. The young are impulsive. And the inheritance represented the sweat and toil of generations.

Yes, said Gil. Generations of people outside his family, who'd labored hard. And gotten pennies for their trouble.

He believed he'd scored a point with that one.

But Hadley only smiled.

During the year to come, he went on, Gil should consider the fact that he would be able to give far more, in the long run, if he continued to hold his assets, donate as much as he liked, and live modestly on a fraction of the dividend and interest income they were generating. He could view himself as merely the keeper of the assets, empowered to disburse them as he saw fit.

You may well come to understand, said Hadley, that this wasn't wealth *hoarding* but philanthropic wealth *management*.

In the end Gil had agreed to the year, though he left the meeting deflated.

His grand gesture had fallen flat. It was as if he'd been pickpocketed.

Afterward he didn't break into a run on sidewalks. Walked at a steady pace like everyone else.

And before the year was up, he met Lane.

When he mentioned his vision of freedom, she read him the riot act. Told him in no uncertain terms that if he gave away everything he'd qualify as an idiot.

Not a moron, not an imbecile, but a full idiot.

The terms were an old-time medical hierarchy. Levels of mental impairment, she said.

She never changed her mind, so he let the rest of the year pass.

And many more after.

"Hell. I wouldn't care if you gave up your money," said Sarah. "Keep the house, though. I really like this place. And maybe a stash to cover the cooling bills."

But it stayed with him, the fact that Dag had to buy his meals at a gas station.

The guy must be haunted by regret. He'd made a mistake when he was young, and in a few seconds his life was taken from him.

"Don't you dare," Sarah said.

THEY DROVE INTO THE MOUNTAINS. It was a long drive up winding roads. Rising steeply from the desert floor, the country turned alpine.

There were pines and other conifers up here, and when they stopped the car by the road and walked into the trees they were beset by noisy, large blue-and-gray jays. The birds followed them along the path, chattering loudly.

Their feet crunched over a bed of brown needles, and the air smelled fresh.

They had dinner at a diner in a small town. Mud on trucks, men wearing cowboy hats. Everyone but them called the waitresses by name. The diner claimed to be known for its chili. On some of the televisions, Fox News was playing. On others it was football.

"Let's just go back to our room," said Sarah.

They'd booked the only place nearby, billed as a "family lodge."

"Already? Even though it has those frilly decorations all over?" he asked. "And the heart-shaped bowls with dried flower petals. What did you call it?"

"Potpourri."

"Even though there was that doll posed sitting on the chair in our room like a person? With the blond braids? The doll that stared at you out of unseeing blue eyes?"

"Still," said Sarah. "In our room, at least there's something to do."

When they got there she turned the doll to face the wall, but the sight of the back of its head was even worse. She said it was a horror movie waiting to happen. She'd stow it in the chest of drawers instead.

With the doll watching, if they happened to fool around, they would for sure be killed.

Stabbed, possibly. Dolls took the sinners first.

JASON CAME TO THE CASTLE'S front door one afternoon with a date. He wasn't the kind to call ahead. He seemed to have brought his date over because he didn't know what else to do.

Gil made them sandwiches and suggested they take a stroll in the wash. It was a mild spring day.

Oh no, said the date. The exposure to plants would trigger her pollen allergies. She could break out in hives. Also, washes were made of sand. And in the sand, various pathogens lay in wait. Hantavirus or valley fever might manifest itself. She'd known a woman once who died.

Gil waited, thinking there was more to the story. But no.

She also had indoor sensitivities. Did he use room deodorizers here? The ones you plugged into outlets? She thought she detected a whiff of artificial citrus.

No room deodorizers, he said. None at all. He could claim, with a clear conscience, that he'd never purchased such an item.

The chemicals in them were a form of biological warfare, said the date. They made the dispensers in the shapes of flowers. Hearts and diamonds! But those dispensers were vessels for poison.

When she entered a bathroom that contained air fresheners, she actually felt cancerous lesions starting to grow inside her lungs. Or her esophagus. She turned around and ran out, when she felt the lesions sprouting. It didn't matter how badly she needed to urinate.

Gil asked if the tumors continued to develop after she fled the polluted bathrooms.

She didn't know, she said. Her jaw was clenched. She *simply didn't know.*

After a while he persuaded her and Jason to take a walk on the pavement. It rarely harbored a disease. Jason glanced back at him as they set off down the sidewalk, and he waved.

Sarah, who liked to mountain-bike in the Superstitions on her days off, settled for riding her road bike crosstown to the castle when she didn't have time to get out of the city. She'd just stowed it in his garage—he watched her coming up the stairs, unclipping her helmet—when the phobic woman reappeared at the front door.

"Help! Help!" she said.

Her body was motionless, but Help! Help! came out of her mouth in a high-pitched squeak.

He and Sarah jogged down the block and found Jason sitting, bent over his knees, on a neighbor's stucco half-wall.

"I couldn't breathe," he said. "Couldn't breathe!"

The worst had passed, it appeared. Sarah didn't have her medical kit with her but sat down on the wall beside him and helped him to breathe slowly. Probably a panic attack, she said.

The phobic woman left right away—they'd come in separate cars, Jason told them after she was gone. In case he was a kidnapper or rapist.

Back at the house Sarah plied him with nonalcoholic beer and asked him what had been going on before the panic attack occurred.

"We were just walking."

"Was there a conversation?" she asked.

"About passenger pigeons. I told her how they used to fill the skies. In their huge flocks that blotted out the sun. And how we hunted them down and burned their trees until they went extinct."

"And?"

"She said pigeons are flying rats. Filthy."

"And then?"

"Something about avian flu? I don't remember."

"Hmm. Well," said Sarah gravely. "Maybe she's not the one for you."

GIL HAD THE HABIT OF skimming his inbox without reading. He'd never got much personal mail. Still less, now that Van Alsten was gone. He used to send the odd piece of satire or news.

Rarely Vic wrote, or Rajiv. But it had been a while.

So it was odd to see Lane's name in the sender column. It looked like a mass email, an announcement of a start-up. A website. Or a business. A business website.

The mass email was personalized. It had his name in the Dear _____ field.

Lane was looking for investors.

She'd sent him a prospectus.

A SPECIES OF RAT once lived on an island in the Indian Ocean. It was a tree-climbing animal, plump and friendly and active, with no fear of humans.

Then sailors arrived, bringing other rats in the hold of their ship. Those rats carried an exotic disease. The local rats had no immunity, so in three decades they had vanished.

A century later it was discovered that a flea had disappeared along with them—a species of flea science had not described. It had lived on those rats alone.

Ted had heard about the flea while driving, on the radio. He and Tom had come over and were sitting with Gil at the living-room bar, Tom eating one of the ice-cream sandwiches Gil kept in the freezer for him.

"That's public radio for you," said Ted. "A story about a flea. And look, I retold it."

"I liked it," said Tom. "No one cares about fleas."

"Except rats," said Gil. "And cats. And dogs."

"And their owners," said Ted.

"But maybe one of those fleas had the best idea ever," said Tom. "Maybe he knew something we don't."

"I strongly doubt it," said his father.

"You can say that," said Tom, shrugging. He'd finished the ice-cream sandwich and had spongy brown pieces of it on his fingers. He picked up the white paper wrapper and licked off a remnant of cream. "But it's just your *opinion*, Dad. You will never, ever know."

JASON DECIDED TO STOP DATING for a while. Celibacy was a lifestyle choice. Just as rewarding as other lifestyle choices.

He used to think he would have been an eagle, if he'd been born a bird. Now he thought he was more of a raven, he told Gil in the shelter's kitchen, eating from a box of snack mix he'd brought with him.

Ravens, like all the corvids, are highly intelligent, he said. Possibly have a theory of mind, even. Can anticipate others' behavior. Solitary, but they stay with a single partner once mated. Both parents take care of the chicks.

Although, he conceded, biologists haven't proved there's no extra-pair copulation.

Raven sex habits were difficult to research. The birds could live for more than fifty years.

"Your raven is a generalist," he explained. "A lot of birders, they like to spot the extreme habitat and dietary specialists. See the rare and endangered species. And sure, me too. But the generalist species—you might call them weedy—are the ones that'll have staying power. In the new world. Like people. And some rats. The specialists, a lot of them are gonna disappear. And birds in general. Since 1970, we've lost almost a third of the whole bird population. Just here in the US of A. Maybe three billion. Read it in *Scientific American*. Goodbye larks, goodbye blackbirds and warblers. Goodbye even to Old World sparrows."

"That's . . ." started Gil. "That's incredibly sad, Jason."

Jason nodded impatiently. It was old news to him.

"You gotta be a generalist, in the new climate. But that's not enough either. If there's too much poison around. We're talking pesticides, mostly. Agrochemicals everywhere. Take the sparrows. So anyways, I'd pick raven. A raven can kill, but will he eat garbage? Yes. He will."

"Good to be flexible."

"And of course, they're clever tricksters. Like the Indians say. True fact: they've been known to peel the labels off barrels of radioactive waste."

"Diabolical," said Gil.

Jason would remain chaste. Saving himself for a lady raven.

Meanwhile he had other worries, because Ricki the guest had it in for him. He didn't know why. He must have done something wrong. Now she followed him around, badgering.

"She just *says* things," he told Gil.

That day they were sitting on the shelter's side-door stoop, looking out into a carport and an oleander bush with bright-pink flowers. Jason dug around in his pocket and pulled out a crushed granola bar.

"Like, what does she say?"

"She says, where did I get my shoes. She didn't know you could buy that kind of Wallabees after the seventies. Or have I tried Hair Club for Men. She says all body shapes are natural so I should be body-positive. But then she laughs."

"For what it's worth," said Gil, "she once called me dickless."

ON THE DAY OF HIS PARTY the castle was overrun by white-shirted caterers. The catering team was a bossy, thin woman, her deferential assistants, and a couple of big, slow guys with shaggy hair who did the heavy lifting. Stoners, Gil thought.

As soon as he could get away Gil took cover in his den. Sat down at his desk and flipped his laptop open, glanced at news items. Scanned his inbox.

There was a message from his lawyer. Dag had written Gil an email, care of the lawyer's email address, which he had forwarded below. The lawyer counseled against reading it, however. It contained sensitive information of a "personal nature." But he felt he had to give Gil the option.

Gil clicked out of the lawyer's email, thought about it.

In the end, curiosity got the better of him.

He went back in. And scrolled down.

Dear Gil. In the Ninth Step we make Amends. I was driving when you're parents got hit and as you know was not sober. Because of the Disease.

I saw a cat crossing the road. I tried to swerve and my truck went up on two wheels. I hit my head on the window. I was dazed but felt the truck scrape on a parked car going pretty fast.

A Couple was on the sidewalk. They were in the shade of trees. Behind a metal sine that said in red letters No Parking. I recall you're Mother had a blue skirt on. Long. They were standing there close.

Could of bin kissing. Not looking up and there faces were in the shade. I only saw them quick.

I should of braked but tried to turn instead but couldn't make the steering work. Front of my truck hit the sine post first and then it crumbled onto the grill and I closed my eyes for a second. And when I opened my eyes the sine was hitting them and the truck to.

So that was how it happened. I hope it helps you get closure.

Signed, "Dag"

Gil sat looking at the words *the sine was hitting them.*

Probably Dag had meant to type "crumpled," but the image that arrived was of a NO PARKING sign disintegrating. Dissolving into particles as it combined itself with the truck, then the parents. A cloud of specks, red letters falling away like clods of dirt.

He sat back and closed his eyes. Tried to clear his mind. But kept seeing the lead-gray metal of a signpost, and then the front of a truck, colliding with the forms of his parents. With their arms around each other, unsuspecting.

Yet their faces were static and posed, the ones from the family portrait. He saw a blue skirt but couldn't fill in the blanks.

Never knew what hit them, his grandmother had said. They'd left him with a babysitter to go out to a movie.

Sudden and without pain.

And could it still be true?

Sudden, anyway.

He'd always assumed his parents had been sitting in a car

when they were hit by another car. On the rare occasions when he hadn't been able to stop himself from trying to picture the event, it was a simple picture of two cars colliding.

His grandmother had first explained it to him after he'd sat watching Saturday morning cartoons. So he conjured up two cartoon cars, a cartoon impact. One car in blue, the other yellow. He hadn't opened up the cars and filled them with parents—he kept it basic. Cartoon cars and waves of impact when they hit.

When he was in his teens he'd added a couple more details to the made-up memory.

A cartoon ambulance.

Cartoon stretchers with cartoon figures on them, prone.

By then the cartoon had turned black and white. The primary colors were gone.

But he'd always worked hard not to picture the injuries. He'd never looked inside the cars.

Then a man he'd never met pushed *send* on an email.

He should have listened to the lawyer.

HE TOSSED BACK a rye before the guests arrived. There was a moment, as they were filing in through the foyer and he was shaking hands with them, when contentment washed over him. Ardis had hung up colored paper lanterns, so he stood in a vault of amber light. Sarah beside him, her arm around his waist.

But for most of the evening a figment trembled at the edge of his sight, a long panel of blue and above it an angular weapon of dull-gray metal. Rectangular white and red.

By two in the morning the caterers had left, and Ted and Ardis. He and Sarah walked through the aftermath: wine and beer spilled on the hardwood floors, pieces of bread ground into throw rugs, remnants of fruit and cheese platters. Scores of half-empty cups arrayed on ledges and windowsills.

A few guests didn't seem ready to go. One of them, a guy leaning against the back of a sofa, seemed to be taunting another. A woman with short, blond hair, wearing a pantsuit. He jabbed at her shoulder with a forefinger and said loudly, accusingly: *Hillary!* Jab. *Hillary!* Jab. *Hillary!* Jab.

"Should I ask him to leave?" he asked Sarah.

She had spots of color high up on her cheekbones. Wine and movement. He thought: She's happy right now.

He wanted her to stay happy. Always.

"Hey. I'm tired. I had three surgeries today. I'm turning in. OK?"

He kissed her and watched her go up the stairs. Then spun on his heel and stood watching from a few dozen paces as the man kept up his caper. He and his companion had moved, and now they were in front of a fireplace, her back against the mantel. She was sipping a drink but held the glass up between them.

"Hey, hi," said Gil, approaching. Addressed himself to her. "Everything OK here?"

She nodded but seemed unconvinced.

"Well. I think we're winding down."

The drunk man turned around. His face looked gray, filmy. Maybe just the sheen of sweat.

"We're *winding down*," he jeered. "We're *winding down*."

The woman looked only at Gil, uncomfortable.

"Let me see you out," he said to her. "Do you live near? Or should I call you a car?"

"I'm really near," said the woman. "I was just getting ready to go, but—"

The drunk crashed his cup down on the mantel, where the liquid slopped over the brim.

She didn't want him tagging along. Clearly.

"I'll see you out."

"I don't fucking need . . ." muttered the drunk.

"I was talking to her, actually," said Gil.

But the man followed as they made their way to the foyer, then stumbled, pitching against a wall.

"Why don't you just wait there," said Gil to him. "I'll be right back."

"Sue your ass," slurred the man. "Sue you. I'll do it. I'll sue it. Faggot."

"Huh."

"Staying," said the man. "Staying."

He slid down against the wall and sat. Head hanging, he slapped at his ankles.

They left him behind.

"He lives on my block," whispered the woman. "He kind of glommed onto me. But I don't really know him."

"I'll take care of it. If you can give me his address."

Gil walked her out. But when he went back inside, the drunk wasn't sitting against the wall anymore. He looked and couldn't find him.

He went up the stairs to join Sarah in the bedroom, stripped off his shirt and shoes and half fell onto the bed.

"Is that guy gone?" she murmured.

"Think so," he said, but lay picturing the man as he wandered the halls beneath them.

Swinging his arms and breaking the furniture.

HAWK

TOM SAID HE COULD FEND OFF future antagonists if he became a martial arts expert. But he wasn't the *best* at combat, he confessed. He got anxious during sparring. What if he hurt someone on accident?

Gil got into a schedule of picking him up from his Thursday class, on his way back from the shelter. He'd sit down to watch the boys punch and kick. Before they aimed their punches and kicks they shouted so loud it rang off the walls: "Yes sir!" "Yes sir!" "Yes sir!"

It seemed paramilitary, but then they all bowed meekly to each other.

Tom didn't like it when his dad dropped him off, because his dad said he was old enough to wait fifteen minutes by himself in the lobby. But while he was waiting he had to see the bald men in the grownup class before him. They came out talking in loud voices and swearing.

He was a bit scared of them, actually.

"What's so scary about a guy with no hair?" asked Gil. "Some men just lose their hair when they get older, right? They can't help it."

Tom said the men weren't *that* old. Plus they had big muscles and lots of tattoos on their arms. Of spiders. And totally naked ladies.

"Totally naked! That's a commitment," said Gil.

SARAH ASKED HIM if he was down. He'd seemed down, ever since the party.

So he told her about the email. How often he saw the scene. The sign bent over the grille of the truck, mowing down his mother.

Mother. Mother. Mother. Pain.

"That Dag's a loose cannon," she said. "Tell the lawyer not to forward any more emails from him."

Gil nodded.

TOM WAS A FREE AGENT again now that school was out again. He would be going back to martial arts day camp at the dojo, he said.

Gil helped him with strength training. There were push-ups and sit-ups, to build his core, Tom said. In the basement he lifted small weights with his spindly arms. Some days the two of them went running together.

On one of these runs—Tom tended to sprint ahead, then quickly become tired and start lagging—they came up behind a man walking and talking. Wearing a baseball cap and a headset. Gil heard "piss-poor margins."

As they passed him Gil glanced to his side, hand up to wave. But then he recognized the face.

It was the angry drunk from the party. Gil's waving hand dropped.

The man didn't look at him. Then they were past.

"That's the kid's dad," said Tom, breathless. "The kid on the bus. His dad!"

"Brad? With the paper clips?"

Tom nodded. "He drops him off. At school."

"I see."

They ran on.

HE CALLED HIS LAWYER and said not to forward more messages. The lawyer said good, he would be glad not to. They'd be filtered into the Crazies folder from now on.

Because Dag had been on a tear lately. Complaining in multiple emails to the lawyer's assistant that he was trying to have "closure" with Gil but "his wife doesn't like me."

Gil was perplexed. He asked Sarah about it.

"You don't defend yourself. I intervened."

"Intervened how?"

"I asked him not to send any more emails. I told him they were damaging to you."

He pondered this.

"It wasn't my business, exactly. I get that."

"Well . . ."

"I texted him at his Skype handle," she said. "Saw it on your screen when he was talking to you. I have kind of—well. It's not eidetic memory. But I remember details."

"OK," he said slowly.

"He's already committed one outrage against your family. And then he hurt you again. In the service of hounding you. For your money."

"I see," he said.

She was right, on the merits.

Yet a small wall had been thrown up between them. He knew it shouldn't be there. But felt the friction of it. A question of boundaries—they weren't clear. Hadn't been defined. It wasn't her fault.

Still, she'd vaulted over one. Without checking in.

That night they moved around each other cautiously.

A FAMILY OF HAWKS lived near the castle. Handsome red-brown birds called Harris's hawks, Jason told him. They hunted together, as a group.

He saw them perched on the top of tall saguaro cacti in his yard, the cacti with raised arms that looked like people. And on electrical poles. He worried about that.

One would dive down and catch a squirrel or cottontail, while the others swooped near. He felt a pang for the prey. But hawks had to eat too.

The largest of them was the mother bird. She also came the

nearest—would alight on a saguaro only a few feet from the edge of his terrace. When he was out there reading or scrolling through newsfeeds on his tablet.

As long as he sat quietly, she'd stay. Making small, jerky movements with her head, looking around.

Sometimes she'd bend her head, her brown eyes bright against her yellow face, and groom her breast or wing feathers with her beak. Tidying.

At those moments he felt they were existing together. Not the same, but side by side. He liked to look at her.

And waited to get up until she'd flown away.

SOON HE FELT himself coming around to Sarah again. She'd done what she'd done out of conviction. Trying to help.

She confronted obstacles head-on. Unlike him. He always steered wide, so wide he could pretend they'd never been there in the first place.

She had his back, he thought.

He wasn't accustomed to someone having his back.

It would take him a while to get used to it.

ARDIS CAME TO THE CASTLE to pick up Tom and motioned Gil over, asked him to come look at something online.

"Not you," she said to Tom. "This is grownup stuff. Keep doing your push-ups."

"But I already did five sets of ten. I'm *finished*. I want to see."

"It's inappropriate," she said firmly.

"Strength training's never finished," said Gil. His interest was piqued. "Do more triceps."

"I *hate* triceps."

In the den Ardis sat Gil down at his laptop and made him bring up the neighborhood website. She pointed to a link called Sign Graffiti!

"Some residents have stuck up campaign signs," she told him. "For the primaries. Though it's still early."

"I saw those."

"Then this happened," said Ardis. She clicked on the link. Photos appeared. Signs on manicured front lawns. The same woman's face on two of them, smiling, the name *Kelly* still legible, and over the smiling face crudely spray-painted shapes in black. One penis, then two penises.

They had roughly drawn testicles, and at the heads, some lines of dashes emerging.

"Dicks? Someone spray-painted *dicks?*"

"You can read the posts. Or I can give you the gist."

"Tell me."

"The dicks are highly offensive, obviously, says one woman. The owners of the houses reported it. Here's a guy who says, Oh, they're just immature. A pissed-off teenager, maybe. And two people say the defacement is hate speech."

"But hate speech is legal anyway. Unless it incites violence."

"Well. The dicks symbolize rape."

"They do? I assumed they were the artist's signature. You know. *I am a dick.*"

"You have to see the backs."

"The backs?"

She scrolled down farther. On the back of one sign were the words *GANG RAPE*. The back of the other read, *Go get raped cunt*.

"Well. That clears up the intent, I guess."

"So now the conversation is, in the neighborhood association, maybe no candidate signs should be allowed."

"The signs? The *signs* are wrong?"

"It's the signs' fault, people say. They're too provocative."

OUT ON A MORNING WALK in the wash, he and Sarah saw a large, dead hawk. Fallen in the sand.

It was the mother. He was almost sure.

She lay on the sand, one wing so loaded with birdshot it had nearly detached from her body.

Gil knelt beside her. Touched the feathers on her back. Then her tail.

There were no ants yet. And no flies. Nothing had found her.

It must have just happened, said Sarah.

She went to get a towel while Gil sat beside the bird. Her large brown eyes were still open. Still bright.

He felt like crying. But then something closed inside him. A hard kernel of anger.

Sarah came back with the towel and he carried the body onto the terrace.

Jason came over to inspect it. Yes, he said. A female. Not a juvenile. Gil was right—likely the matriarch.

There was no raptor-hunting season, Jason said. You were never supposed to shoot raptors. They were protected by law. This included eagles, falcons, and hawks.

"So quail hunting is legal," said Gil. "But this isn't. Right?"

"You could report it to Game and Fish," said Jason. "Or the feds. But they won't do anything. Unless you know who it was. They wouldn't prosecute. Hunters are those guys' bread and butter. It's just a fine, anyway."

"It was the same person who shot the quail, I bet," said Sarah. "The same MO. Leaving them there."

Tom came running up the back stairs, carrying his black bag of sparring gear. He was proud of the bag. He brought it over even when he had no intention of practicing. Carried it like a briefcase. A professional with his kit.

"Oh," he said, seeing the bird. Dropped his bag.

"It's the mother hawk who used to visit me," said Gil. "The family that catches things in the wash."

"Someone shot her, honey," said Sarah.

Tom stared down. "Poor hawk."

"Yeah," said Gil.

"We have to bury her."

They dug a hole in the backyard.

HE MADE A THIRD sortie. A fourth and fifth and sixth. Stayed out for longer. Once, sat down on a soft swell of sand. He'd taken a thermos of coffee with him.

But caught only himself. Nodding off.

AT THE END OF HIS SHIFT at the shelter that Friday the director called him in for a talk. She shut the door behind them and gestured at the visitor's chair. He sat.

Felt like a kid in the principal's office. He respected the director. A straight talker. Didn't mince her words.

"Look, you've been great," she said. "You're very popular. With the board *and* the guests. Except for Ricki, maybe. But you know. She doesn't like anyone. Man *or* woman."

"But?"

"There's a concern, right now. Among the members of the board. The culture in the country. The president, et cetera. The toxic masculinity."

"Well," he said. "Yeah. It is pretty toxic."

"And they've decided, until the gender climate improves, to put the Friendly Man program on hold."

"The Friendly Man?"

"It's the official name. We use it in our fund-raising documents. For the male volunteer project."

"I see."

He was a Friendly Man.

"I want you to know, it wasn't my decision. I'm just an employee, not a board member. Don't have a vote. And the feeling of the board is, the women are living under a constant threat. These women, our guests, there's no larger support system for them. The thinking is, in this small haven from that broader toxicity, we're going to need to follow a more conventional model, for a while. Use female escorts. The shelter has to be an all-female space."

"I understand."

"I wanted to get you guys a cake, let the guests say goodbye properly. But the board nixed it. They don't want to make the transition into, you know, a *thing*."

No more Friendly Men.

Jason would take it harder. His position made him proud.

"You'll be the first to know if the policy changes back," said the director, as he got up to leave. "We'll miss you around here."

WITH THE NEW GAP in his schedule Gil had time on his hands. He made calls about other volunteer posts, but return calls came in slowly.

Jason was always inviting him out and he was always declining. So one night when Sarah was at the hospital he agreed to meet. There was a karaoke bar Jason went to. It was dark and had country-western stylings. Elderly couples danced two-steps and polkas on the floor.

"I've never performed," admitted Jason.

They sat near the stage, where the music was loud and they almost had to yell to hear each other.

"This is your coming-out party, then," said Gil. "Get up there! You can do it."

Jason demurred, but Gil urged him. If he didn't come here to drink, and they couldn't talk, at least he had to sing. So Jason put his name on a list and after a while took the mic.

He faltered at the beginning but was strong on the chorus. "You picked a fine time to leave me, Lucille. With four hungry children and a crop in the field."

There was a smattering of applause, and when he sat down he seemed gratified.

"See?" said Gil. "Not too bad, right?"

He enjoyed watching the old folks dance. He nursed his pint of beer.

And he got home late. Unlocking his door, fumbling with the keys because the bulb in the front light was out, he noticed headlights in the street behind him.

It was Ardis's car. She didn't stay out late much unless she was out with friends. And when she went out late with friends she always took a car home. Or got a ride from one of them. Or made Ted pick her up.

But he was across the Pacific. Away on a business trip for three weeks.

Gil went inside and couldn't stop himself from glancing out a window as she entered the glass house. She wore heels and a cocktail dress, and her hair was already down. That too was unusual. Ardis was a creature of habit.

Working late, he guessed.

But typically when she had extra work she brought her laptop back to the house. Clem could babysit Tom, but she preferred not to.

And Ardis tried not to be the last to leave her office, she'd told him. She hadn't mastered the alarm system.

Still. It was none of his business.

FLICKERS

WITH TED GONE he was in charge of picking up Tom from his day camp three times a week, while Ardis was getting Clem from her dance class. One afternoon he and Sarah went to the dojo with a carful of groceries. They'd started shopping together, planning their meals.

She was consulting on a case over the phone, so he left her on the call and went in.

Tom was sparring. Gil sat down at the viewing window to watch. There was a beefy, crew-cut guy presiding. Gil didn't recognize him. Instead of a white uniform he wore a tight black T-shirt and sweats.

At first Gil's focus was on Tom, barely holding his own against his partner. An older girl.

But then his attention was diverted. The counselor was

between Gil and Tom and did a fist pump when the girl landed a punch. As he raised his arm the tight sleeve of his T-shirt rode up, and a tattoo showed.

Gil turned away from the window and went out to the lobby, where a young woman with a ponytail sat behind the desk. High-gloss lips. Coming around from the side, he saw she was playing a bright, pastel-colored game on her cell.

"I'm here to pick up one of your campers," he said.

"Uh-huh? There's fifteen minutes left."

"But I'm wondering, who's the guy who's teaching them right now? I haven't seen him here before."

"He's a sub," she said. "Three counselors called in sick."

"I'd like to know his name, please."

She put down her cell and turned to the computer. Tap-tapped.

"I'm pulling up the schedule. Right, Ryan. He's trained here for a while. He's definitely qualified. A black belt. You don't need to worry."

"It's not his skills I'm worried about," said Gil. "It's the tattoo on his arm. Are you aware?"

"Well, we don't have a policy against *tattoos*," said the woman, chuckling. Then smiling at him winningly. "Or we wouldn't have any members." She swiveled in her chair and pulled down her shirt collar to expose a colorful shoulder. Blues and greens. A blond mermaid riding a leaping dolphin.

"Very nice. But his isn't a mermaid. It's a swastika."

She swiveled back.

"Oh," she said. Her face was blank. "Are—are you Jewish?"

He was briefly speechless.

"What does *that* have to do with it?"

"I mean. I guess . . . like, no. I didn't see. We don't, like, vet people's tats. You know?"

She bit her shiny bottom lip.

"You have a guy with a swastika on his body teaching children," said Gil. "Children are in there saying *Yes sir* to a neo-Nazi. You don't think that's a problem?"

"I mean. I don't, like, do the *hiring*. Or whatever."

"I'm Gil, by the way. What's *your* name?"

"It's Brandi. With an *i*."

"I'll be taking my kid now, please, Brandi."

Shorthand. He was approved for pickup, that was all she had to know. There was a file with approved names. A sign-in and sign-out sheet. He picked up the pen and found Tom's name.

"Like, yeah, sure," she said.

"Would you go in and get him for me, please?"

They locked the door between the observation room and the gym space. Security, they said. There was a code on it. But the code didn't keep out Nazis.

"OK. Hold on."

He waited.

Tom came out carrying his black net bag and looking impatient. Brandi was behind him.

She touched her ponytail self-consciously. Slipped the elastic off and smoothed her hair back to redo it.

"How come I have to leave early?" he said. "It was just getting good! Did you see?"

"Tell you later."

Tom slid into the backseat of the car, next to some bags of groceries. "How come you made me leave?" he asked again, plaintive.

"Hey, martial arts expert!" said Sarah. She'd finished her call. "How was your camp today?"

"He made me leave *early*," complained Tom.

"There was a leadership issue," said Gil, and poked the car's power button.

He felt Sarah looking at him sidelong.

At the glass house Tom retired to his room.

Sometimes he didn't like to be in the *middle* of everything, he'd told Gil once.

Ardis got a bottle of wine and the three of them went out onto the back patio. Sat.

"Shoot," said Ardis.

"Yeah, shoot," said Sarah. "The suspense is killing me."

So he told them as they drank.

"The receptionist did say he's a sub," he said. "They had a staff shortage today. So he's not there all the time."

"Maybe he's a *reformed* skinhead," said Ardis, hopeful. "I met a guy like that. Now he's a shrink. Heads this nonprofit that reaches out to extremists. Re-education. He focuses on what drives people to hate groups. Parental and family abandonment. A lack of positive role models."

"Reformed? Then why would he still have the tat?" said Sarah.

"Anyway, I took Tom out. I got the guy's first name."

"Damn," said Ardis, shaking her head. "He's so attached to going there."

"Maybe just ask the management," said Sarah. "They may have no idea. I mean, we shouldn't discount the possibility it's just an oversight. Sheer incompetence."

"I have no idea how they vet their staff," said Ardis. "It was Ted that found the place. For all I know, he based the choice on Yelp reviews."

"I've treated neo-Nazis," said Sarah. "One patient told me he wanted to exterminate the Jews. He said it was his duty to the Brotherhood. He had a broken bottle stuck in his stomach at the time. So I cut him some slack. But I did tell him two of his three surgeons were Jewish. I said, You better not murder the Jews in *this* room. Or that old hunk of glass is going to be the end of you."

"Jesus," said Ardis.

"I remember the label like it was yesterday—Schnapps. *Butterscotch.*"

She shuddered.

Maybe it was just the training she'd had. Med school. Or long experience. But he admired her equanimity.

It wasn't as if she was a neutral party. Two of her grandparents, Ashkenazi Jews, had died in the Holocaust.

"I'll call the head counselor in the morning," said Ardis. "See what he says. Thanks for dealing, Gil."

He finished his wine. Ardis would take care of it. She was dependable.

So she'd come in late one night. It was hardly illegal.

No Parking signs were everywhere. It was what they were made for. Wherever he went, there they were.

And then his mother came to mind. His father too, but his mother first.

He didn't remember love, but he imagined it.

When he was little, he had relied on this imagining, alone in his bed at night. A comforting projection. Being held in her arms. Warm and safe.

That was gone now. Whenever he saw a sign he saw the truck bearing down and felt a flash of her fear.

The fear was their new connection.

Gil had looked up the Ninth Step: the AA literature said you weren't supposed to "make amends" when doing so might hurt someone. Either Dag hadn't understood his confession would do that or he didn't give a shit.

Whether he was malicious or only dim-witted, the root cause had to be need. The guy was desperate.

So Gil decided to submit. Dag would receive a weekly stipend. Not lottery winnings, but enough to live on decently. Enough to allow him to take a bus or car to a grocery store. And buy real food.

In exchange, he'd never contact Gil or the lawyer again.

"Besides the fact that you're basically rewarding a guy for bad behavior, it sets a terrible precedent," said Hadley. "First off, the man's a drug addict. Odds are he'll spend it on something cut with fentanyl and OD within the week. A classic case of misplaced charity. Not your first rodeo, Gil."

Hadley had been his only constant, over the years. He was white-haired now. His grandchildren were getting married. Soon the constant would be gone.

And he wasn't wrong. He was never wrong—only irritatingly reasonable.

"Still, though. The money means more to him than me. He's old and sick. So let's just give him some."

"Why do you have a soft spot for this individual? Beyond the obvious facts of the case, he's a loser and a user. Always was, as I recall."

"I can't stand the guy. I just want to be rid of him."

Hadley's sigh was clear. All the way from Manhattan. "Let it be noted that I do this under protest," he said.

"Noted."

He was ashamed, slightly, he realized after the call. A lazy solution, his form of self-defense: throw money.

But it was better thrown. He felt a little lighter.

IN ONE OF HIS BACKYARD'S tallest saguaros a woodpecker lived in a hole. They called them flickers, this kind of woodpecker.

Only the flickers built the nesting holes. But then the holes were used by many other birds, he read. Freeloaders, in a way. Finches and sparrows, flycatchers and wrens. Elf and screech owls.

When the flickers were nesting and you walked near, they poked their heads out of the holes and issued loud, piercing alarm calls.

ONE NIGHT IN BED with Sarah next to him he woke up at 3 a.m. Lay there for a while and then got up. Quietly: she was a light sleeper. Even him turning and pulling the sheets over could wake her up.

He padded down the stairs. Went into the kitchen for a seltzer and flicked on the light. Stood at the window over the sink, looking at the night. A lake of darkness.

He popped the tab on the can and sipped from it, gazing out at nothing.

Then lights flicked on. Startled him. In the glass house living room. Ardis was coming in the front door. Her hair was down again.

He stood still, the seltzer can at his lips.

She walked across the room, dumped a shoulder bag on a sofa's end table. Walked across her glass stage. And then her head turned. She saw him.

She stopped walking. There was something in it, her cessation of motion. She was a caught person.

They both stood there. He in his small rectangle of light, she in her large one. Then she raised her hand slowly.

But didn't wave. Just held it there.

He raised his own. After a moment she turned and went down the hall to her bedroom.

SCREECH

TED GOT HOME from his trip, and Gil saw him a couple of evenings in a row for whiskey on the terrace.

To work with his Japanese colleagues, he'd had to learn the different bows. He sometimes mixed them up, prompting politely restrained mirth. With the Chinese coworkers there was a list of banned conversation subjects, supplied in a memo by the HR department. Those banned subjects included Lady Gaga and Katy Perry. Also Justin Bieber.

An engineer from Singapore had gotten drunk at a dinner and proclaimed the end of America. The empire was dying, he said, waving his glass around. Maybe it was already dead.

America had once ruled the earth, he said. But it had never bothered to educate its people. So now it was a country of ignorant peasants, a noisy and stupid rabble.

They shit on science. They shit on the future.

Other colleagues had hurried him off into a taxi, highly apologetic.

He wasn't accustomed to alcohol, they explained.

Worried the guy might get fired, or even worse, Ted did his best to reassure them.

In wine is truth, he said.

TOM HAD BEEN ALLOWED to finish the boot camp—there'd only been two days left—and passed his belt test. He played at the castle most days, while his parents went to work. Practiced his forms and combinations in the basement, wearing the new belt.

It was hot and still. The monsoon season was coming. Gil used his swamp cooling system, opened the windows to let the moisture blow through the castle and cool it. He liked the moving air.

When the rains came it would be too humid for this. He would have to shut the windows and use the AC.

He dreamed of Ted and Ardis. A predictable dream. His dreams were often so obvious they didn't require interpreting.

They stood on the sidewalk where his parents had been, hit by the falling sign. Gil was behind the steering wheel, and Tom was in the backseat, scared.

But Gil's hands never touched the wheel, only clung to his chest, balled into fists. The wheel spun, turning the car on its own.

CONNIE CALLED and said she was building a basketball court. Up in Harlem. The paved lot where Van Alsten used to play was being converted to condos, so the community needed a new court.

It would be public. For the guys he'd played with. And anyone else who wanted to use it.

Would Gil come to the dedication? Labor Day weekend. It would double as Van Alsten's memorial. Maybe he could say a word or two.

I'll be there, he promised.

ON A SATURDAY Ardis appeared at his back door. She carried her pitcher of hummingbird nectar. Sarah was working so he was by himself.

"Tom and Ted are out at that place where kids jump around on indoor trampolines," said Ardis. "Can I rinse out the feeder in your kitchen? It really needs it."

"Much obliged," he said.

But he felt out of sync with her. They hadn't talked since he saw her come in that night. The night before Ted's return.

He stood across the room as she washed the feeder. It was glass, with a red bottom and yellow flowers. Those flowers were for people's benefit, she said. The birds were only drawn to the red.

"I've heard that too," he said.

"Listen," said Ardis, turning. "I'm sorry."

"Sorry for what?"

"For putting you in that position."

"What—oh."

"I guess we should get that wall re-tinted. Finally."

"Well. The waiting list."

"Yeah. I may have let that go a bit. You have to keep calling them."

"But anyway. I didn't *know*. Till now."

"Yes you did. I saw your face. You knew. Because you know me."

"I guess I do," he said slowly.

"I'll just say it's over."

"Oh," he said again. "Good."

He was disappointed that he'd been correct in his cheap suspicion. Felt a tinge of something like aggrievement. As though it was him that she'd cheated on.

But also relieved. It was in the past, she'd said.

So it wouldn't be a threat to Ted.

"It won't happen again. It was something I did for—call them perverse reasons. Emotionally perverse."

"You don't have to explain yourself to me," he said quickly. The truth was he didn't want to hear.

"Oh, I know."

She turned back to the counter and set the feeder on it. Picked up the pitcher and poured.

"We'll be OK now," she said. "Ted and I."

"I hope so. Good."

"We will. Trust me. I only did it to help me forget something else."

And when she turned around again and looked him in the eyes, a shock went through him.

Then she walked past, bird feeder in one hand and pitcher in the other.

He stood there. Heard the *tuck* of the sliding door to the terrace as it closed. The seal of its vacuum.

He had a sensation of hovering in an unseen wake. As though he'd been left in the slipstream of her moving body.

Doubt. Disorientation.

Then dismissal.

The door was closed behind her. Softly but firmly.

THAT EVENING, from the window over his desk, he saw a family of screech owls on a mesquite tree. Five of them. Each sitting on a different branch but facing the same way. Small birds about the size of a fist, the color of brown-gray bark.

The screech owls were well camouflaged. If he hadn't been gazing into the branches, he wouldn't have made them out. They sat and stared back at him out of their yellow eyes, occasionally blinking.

Or stared in his general direction. Quite possibly they didn't see him.

He was unsettled. He realized he'd idolized Ardis. It was unrealistic, what he expected from her.

She wasn't Lane. She wasn't a deserter. She was devoted to her husband. And her children.

Ted had said it himself: it was only fair.

But why could no one be steadfast? Just stay?

HE SELDOM WENT OVER to Sarah's place. More and more, she didn't either.

She preferred the castle, she said. Its cavernous rooms, its crown molding. Who wouldn't?

She kept some clothes in a spare closet off his bedroom, a walk-in he'd never used since all his clothes fit in a smaller one. Except for his shoes, which sat on a low shelf there. He wandered into the walk-in while he was packing for the memorial trip and realized he liked seeing her things hanging. But there was room for more.

Maybe when they got back he could float the notion of her renting out her bungalow for a time. Moving in with him.

On the other hand, she didn't need the rental income. It might seem premature. Cloying.

In New York, Lane used to say, love was a function of real estate. Even upper-middle-class couples moved in together out of pure economy. The high overhead of every apartment.

And stuck together for the same reason.

At the time, he hadn't suspected she meant her. And him.

HE AND SARAH stayed at a hotel off Gramercy Park. The hotel had a trendy bar, popular on weekends. The bar was "selective" about who got past the doorman, said the receptionist, giving them a sales pitch as they checked in. But if they wanted to be sure of entry, they could reserve a table, she told them.

There was a nonrefundable fee of nine hundred dollars for the reservation.

"Nine hundred *dollars*?" asked Sarah, low. "Is this a hotel for assholes?"

It was almost a whisper. Gil felt a slight embarrassment. Worried that the receptionist might have heard.

Behind the desk, she smiled austerely and handed back Gil's credit card.

Why, yes it is, she seemed to be saying. Welcome.

Gramercy Park was a private, leafy enclosure for residents of the square, as well as hotel guests. If you wanted to visit it, you had to have a doorman walk you over and open the door to the park gate with his key. Then you were locked in until you called the doorman's cell and asked him to let you out again.

"It's like a prison, but with trees," said Sarah. "What if the doorman's busy?"

"I guess you wait?"

He'd always been curious about the park. It had a quietly mythic quality.

"No thank you. I'm from Texas. To me it doesn't feel like luxury to be at the mercy of a doorman."

So they would look at it from the outside, like the rest of Manhattan.

HE WAS JITTERY the next morning. Had never made a speech. Back in school he'd even avoided making presentations in his classes, so deeply had the prospect of public speaking alarmed him.

As it did most of his fellow Americans.

Sarah wasn't bothered by it. She often gave talks at conferences. And to groups of students and residents.

"Just go off the cuff," she said.

Seeing his face, she laughed.

He'd written his remarks on cue cards and memorized them carefully. In the hotel room she sat behind an antique desk in a white hotel robe and slippers and offered to listen to him rehearse.

"No, no, and no," he said.

Instead he ran through it in the shower. Van Alsten hadn't been one for sentimentality. He would have wanted humor. But of all of the mourners, Gil only knew Vic—and Connie, a little. It had been hard to decide, when he was thinking what to say, whether to speak toward the two of them or to the ghost of Van Alsten.

According to Ted, at least half of their fellow Americans believed in ghosts. There'd been several polls on the subject. Ghosts or spirits of the dead, was what they believed in.

Ted had learned about this widespread belief during the cultural-sensitivity training before his Asia trip. In Japan the figure was even higher. In Japan they had many categories of ghosts.

There were mother ghosts who died in childbirth and came back to bring their babies gifts. The ghosts of martyrs. The ghosts of those who died at sea. The mischievous ghosts of children.

On the matter of public speaking, Gil was united with his fellow citizens. On the matter of ghosts, less so.

The ceremony was being held near sundown. This meant he

had a long day to dread it. Sarah would distract him with tourist activities.

He said he wasn't a tourist—he was a lapsed New Yorker. It was like a lapsed Catholic, but without the guilt. Mostly.

Well, *I'm* a tourist, she said. And *I* want to go up in the goddamn Empire State Building.

Before the ceremony she would buy him a stiff drink.

HE'D TAKEN THE SUBWAY a lot when he lived in the city. Always felt swept up in the hurrying crowds, the busy vectors of other lives. He liked the grimy tiles, the soaring metal struts. It was a great and noble work.

But Sarah thought the timing was risky, and they were in midtown already. He skipped the part where he could tell her that trains were actually more reliable than cars during rush hour and shrugged his acquiescence. They got in a cab after their drinks and he felt her clutching his hand, then realized it was him doing the clutching.

He made himself relax his grip.

Don't be unmanly, his grandmother had once snapped at him when he grabbed her hand in public. He'd been shying away from some lurching passerby. Harvard Square, maybe? Cambridge, anyway. He remembered the red brickwork.

He'd been maybe seven or eight and not aspiring to be manly. Her embarrassed rebuke had confused him.

But now it had to be stipulated: he *was* a man. By the numbers, at least.

Then act like it, said his grandmother in his head.

When they reached the address, after sitting awhile in stopped crosstown traffic, calm descended on him. Not the elevated calm of peace—more the fatalistic calm of a condemned person.

The scene was idyllic. There were kids running around. The new basketball court was surrounded by trees. Ginkgoes with their dappled light, soaring maples casting a broad shade.

Outside the court there was a playground. Kids slid down slides, scrambled up a fresh new climbing wall with colorful plastic handholds.

Inside the court were rows of folding chairs and a crowd milling. A podium was set up in front of the seats with a lectern and mic.

The sight turned his stomach, so he looked away.

At the opposite end of the court was the basketball hoop. Festooned with flowers. Behind it, at the base of the fence, was a makeshift altar.

He and Sarah walked up and looked at the tributes. Photos of Van Alsten, from glossy family portraits to candid pictures that looked like they'd been printed out from phone cameras. Bouquets and candles and homemade signs.

V.A. WE LUV U MAN.

V.A. FOREVER!

U LIVE IN MY HEART.

He saw the paper flowers from the hospital. Vic's rosary hung on the corner of a framed shot of Van Alsten smiling, wearing his Yale shirt. Young and toned. Holding a basketball.

Another one of him in his Navy uniform.

He looked around at the people milling. Many of them, if the ghost statistic could be believed, thought they might be visited one day by Van Alsten's translucent figure. Shimmering from the folds of a curtain. Lifting a vodka tonic in a comfortable chair.

The ghost of a man who'd given his body.

Personally, he'd be delighted to learn that ghosts were real. Then he could see Van Alsten again.

And hope, one day, to meet his parents.

He'd welcome it with open arms—proof of a miracle. That a soul could be set free from a body. The souls might gather in a host, flock together and wheel and spin. Funnel and disperse.

"Gil!" said Connie.

She looked better. Not so thin. Her face was shining. He introduced her and Sarah.

"So many people!" said Sarah.

"It turned out he *did* have a lot of friends, after all," said Connie to Gil, and smiled. "Just not in the part of town we lived in. But it's OK. I know them now."

He sat beside Sarah as the rest of the crowd slowly began to settle. There was talk and motion, and the seating seemed to be taking forever. The fatalistic calm receded, inconveniently. It was replaced by nervousness.

He knew he should feel otherwise, but he wanted it to be done. One of his legs was jiggling and he stilled it, but then his arms started to tremble.

Unmanly! he thought, angry at his own arms.

"Hey," whispered Sarah. She held the arm next to her, applying a firm pressure. "Don't worry. Look. It's just good you said yes. For Connie's sake. It'll be fine. And then it'll be over."

He tried to listen to Connie's eulogy but missed parts of it, running over his own. He did hear her say Van Alsten hadn't been squeaky clean. They all knew that, she said. He drank too much and swore like a sailor. Which he had been, of course. Though, in the end, he'd spent more time on land than sea.

Van Alsten must have had a military burial, Gil realized. The triangle-folded flag and the playing of Taps.

He had to ask Connie where the grave was. And pay a visit.

Before his tours, when he was very young, he'd been one man, said Connie. She'd known him then too. At thirty he came home for good, and he was another. That was when the drinking had begun. He seldom spoke of the war, didn't want to burden others, but constantly suffered from restless sleep. After his tours were over, not a day went by when he didn't think of those who were still serving.

In one conflict or the next.

Or those he'd served with who'd fallen.

He had survivor's guilt. When she got sick, he'd never hesitated to help her.

He hadn't been spotless, but he had been good. He said one thing and did another.

That was the thing about Van Alsten. Beneath the armor, he had always been good.

His son stood and spoke but got choked up; his daughter cut her own off mid-sentence with "Thank you." She went to sit by her mother, who put an arm around her.

Van Alsten's brother spoke. Stilted but heartfelt.

Then it was Gil.

He got up on shaky legs and told his small stories, the one about Van Alsten's first night at the refugee center, how the kids were startled by his foul language but soon became his loyal acolytes. How they followed him around during and after the games like little pilot fish in the wake of a big, friendly shark. And then he told the anecdote about the pigeon.

The mourners laughed at that. Even harder than the joke deserved.

They wanted to laugh, he realized. Simple.

He finished. He could relax. The weight was lifted.

Legs spoke next. He was stocky and very short. Hence the nickname. He told of Van Alsten's ridiculous generosity, as he called it. He was V.A. or Van to them.

Van didn't pull his punches. Didn't poor-mouth. People respected him for it. He said he was a rich white guy and fuck if he could help it. He took them out to a restaurant every week after the Friday game.

He offered to treat them to snobby places, Legs said, places where the food cost a shitload, as much as some of the guys' weekly pay. Van Alsten said, Don't look at the prices. The Man is paying! This is your chance to gouge him!

They tried one of those restaurants to humor him, but sorry, they didn't like it. The food was weird, and there wasn't enough of it either. As the joke went. One doll-sized plate came with a spoonful of some brown mushy shit, and then a sprig of grass on it. Hand to God, he told the audience. Actual *grass*. We thought it was a joke. Like Van was playing a trick on us. And they'd bring in the real food next.

But no, we were supposed to eat it. After that we always made him take us to the same burger joint.

The audience laughed and clapped, made appreciative comments.

Then Connie was up again and said there'd be a brief tribute at the hoop. Guests could swivel their chairs. She gave them a minute to do it.

It was getting dark, and the lights on the court stayed off. The hoop alone was lit, a ring of Christmas lights twinkling beneath the flowers.

On one side of the court players lined up, each holding his own basketball. In the dimness the basketballs glowed. Different colors, green and yellow and blue and white.

"How do they do that?" murmured Gil.

"Spray paint," whispered Sarah. "Glow-in-the-dark. I saw them piled under a work light at the fence. I wondered why. Charging, I guess."

"For you, Van," yelled Legs. He was first in line. He took a shot, and his green-and-white ball swished through the net. Then the next guy went. Basket after basket. One guy did a layup. None of them missed.

Kids got up from the chairs, and a couple ran in from the playground. The men handed them the basketballs, and they shot too. When they missed they collected the bouncing balls sheepishly and lined up to try again.

The court lights came up, and it turned into a game.

THERE WAS A WAKE at a local bar. The ballplayers all changed out of their sneakers for it. They'd worn them on the court and then switched.

Honoring Van Alsten's personal bar dress code.

Legs told Gil that had been a tough one to organize. A lot of the younger guys hadn't owned any shoes that weren't sneakers. Sneaker meant shoe, and shoe meant sneaker.

At the counter, waiting for drinks to arrive to take back to the booth he was sharing with Vic and Inez and Sarah, he noticed a couple of men in dress uniform next to him. They held their white hats under one arm and used their other arm to lift their drinks.

He wondered if there was a rule against putting the hats down.

"Good eulogy," said the one facing him.

The other turned.

"Yeah, man," he agreed. "You got Van to a T."

"Thanks," he said. "It was pretty painful. I don't do public speaking. I'm Gil, by the way."

They introduced themselves. Rick and Duane.

"I was gonna say something, maybe," said Rick. "But then I got cold feet."

"Well, I *almost* did."

"I would've made a fool of myself. Blubbering."

"So you served with him?"

Gil's drinks came and he fumbled in his wallet for a tip.

"He never talked about how it was," said Gil. "The war part. Only about the people he knew there."

"Yeah, you know," said Duane. He had a strong southern

accent. "You don't want to relive it. Most times. And not with folks that weren't there."

"One time we lost almost the whole team," said Rick. "But it wasn't down to him. He always went the extra mile, Van did. Took fucking *insane* risks. We always said it was a miracle he got out in one piece."

"He'd do anything for his guys," agreed Duane.

"We're the only SEALs left now," said Rick. "From this one Taliban ambush."

"He was a stone-cold hero," said Duane. "If you hadda been there, you wouldn't have believed some of the shit he pulled."

They nodded, musing.

Rick let out a bark of laughter. "What you said about the swearing. We always figured he had Tourette's. Because that's what he'd do in the field. Just this full-auto stream of four-letter words. Everyone has a foul mouth in combat. But with him it was like rifle fire. Like he was covering us. By shooting out this, like, volley of fucks and bitches."

"He had some weird ones, too," said Duane, nodding. "You remember? They'd make you smile when nothing was funny. Made-up stuff. Like assdigger. Assbandit."

"Asscannon. Nosefuck."

"Shit, man, we need to keep it down."

An older man behind them was looking on in disapproval.

BEFORE THEY LEFT they sat with Connie for a while.

"Actually," said Gil, "there *is* something I've been wanting to ask you."

"Oh?"

"It's something he would never tell me," he said. "Point-blank refused. So maybe it's still out of bounds."

"You can ask me anything."

"What was his first name? The one he hated so much?"

Connie leaned close. "Octavian."

EGG

IT WAS HER LAST YEAR trick-or-treating, Clem had told her parents. She'd be going as a dark angel.

"Dark like evil?" asked Gil.

"I think more like, just wearing a black outfit," said Ted. "Not sure she's too interested in the moral dimension."

"So she won't act the part."

"No more than usual, I guess. She's not into the goth look normally. Condemns it in no uncertain terms. But she likes the eye makeup. Watches video tutorials. How to do smoky eyes."

"Her last trick-or-treat, huh?"

"End of childhood."

They were driving around on a scouting trip, checking out new dojos. Ted had performed reconnaissance on the old one, sneaking into the observation room to check out an adult class. The students were not suffering from male-pattern baldness:

multiple heads were shaved. Hairstyles weren't damning, he said, and he'd spotted no more swastikas.

Still, determined not to go home empty-handed, he took pictures in the small parking lot.

Two jacked-up trucks, parked side by side. One with a Confederate battle flag, the other's hood painted with a black-and-white circle and cross. Celtic.

"Stormfront logo," Ted had said. "I had to look it up."

Whether it was just one guy or something more they couldn't know. But either way, Tom was switching.

He was going to dress up as a pirate.

"Old school!" said Gil. "Not one of those Somali pirates, I'm guessing?"

"A hybrid deal," said Ted. "He asked for a tricornered hat. And a jacket and cuffed boots like Jack Sparrow. But no sword. Instead of a sword he wants to carry his Nerf blaster."

It was a peer-group fad. Ardis had several rules against gunplay, including the one about video games. But her father, a kindly old widower with dementia who lived alone and far away, had forgotten the rules. He'd bought Tom a large blaster. Put considerable effort into buying and sending the gift. And requested photos of his grandson playing with it.

Then one thing led to another.

The blaster looked like a plastic AK-47, except that it was bright orange.

Tom had wished to spray-paint it black for a zombie-themed blaster game with his friends. On someone's birthday.

Listen, there's a reason that they don't manufacture them in the colors of real guns, Sarah warned.

"You play outside sometimes, right? There might be a cop around to get nervous and shoot you. In your neighborhood, it'd be one of those rent-a-cops. I've run into more than a few security guards with stupidly light trigger-fingers. Do me a solid. Don't paint it black. Or even gray."

She'd operated on several young shooting victims.

Tom feared his mother's judgment. He insisted the toy wasn't a gun.

"It's not a gun, it's a *blaster*," he told Gil earnestly.

"Ah. I see," nodded Gil. "Yes, interesting, hmm. Its resemblance to a gun is uncanny."

It fired shell-like projectiles in rapid succession. Tom ran around shooting them off in Gil's basement, which he selected for its space and lit-up pinball targets. As well as its convenient distance from his mother. Gil was constantly finding the spent ammo in nooks and crannies. Once a shell—which Tom called a dart—showed up in his laundry basket after going through the dryer, its blue foam shredded into the cups of bras and the crotches of underwear.

Blaster tolerance divided along gender lines: Gil and Ted were willing to turn the other cheek, but Ardis and Clem were contemptuous of the habit.

When they showed their contempt, Tom was hurt. He didn't like to be suspected of aggression.

The blaster was just *fun*, he protested tearily, when the subject was brought up over dinner.

And ran off. Tragically misunderstood.

"The thing is, guns *qua* guns are not OK," said Ted. "See that? D'you see what I was doing there? Latin! I *did* learn something in college. But maybe we should go easy on him. About the gunplay. I mean, the martial arts stuff is all about forms. And a bit of self-defense. Truth is, my boy wouldn't harm a fly."

"Or an ant," said Gil. "When he sees an ant in the house, he takes it out to the garden. Won't even kill a mosquito."

There were more of these in the neighborhood than there used to be, an old-timer had told Ardis. Though less water was being used.

"I personally saw him being bitten by a mosquito and refusing to slap it," Gil went on. "He just waited and let it finish biting him."

Tom was reading a book about the lives of insects and often lectured Gil on its contents. He said they were in global decline and had to be saved.

Mosquitoes, though? said Gil. They spread disease. Malaria, for one.

Not here, said Tom.

Well then, West Nile, said Gil.

Just because insects were small and didn't have brains didn't mean they didn't have thoughts and feelings, said Tom. Decentralized nervous systems. A different setup from brains, but very effective.

"An ant could be smarter than *you* are," he'd said sternly. "You're smaller than a blue whale, aren't you? A *lot* smaller, Gil. But I bet you think you're smarter than a blue whale is."

"Jury's still out. Science-wise. *Orcas* could easily be smarter than me. I know that much. Maybe the smaller dolphins. And probably elephants, too."

"Gil. FYI. Some ants? They actually help their friends."

After one dinner with a blaster-related conflict, the adults sat on the back porch having drinks. Clem came out to show off her angel costume. A VIP preview, she called it.

She did everything in advance. Clem was organized.

She wore a tight-fitting black bodysuit with a ghostly white skeleton shape on it. Her wings were black too. Elaborately feathered.

"You *do* look evil," said Ardis.

"Did they kill crows to get those things?" asked Ted.

"Do they *murder* the crows?" said Sarah.

She liked puns, Gil had noticed. He'd ribbed her about it. A character flaw, she admitted.

And he'd said: Well. He could live with it. She didn't have many of them.

"Daddy. They're *dyed*."

"Oh. Maybe they killed geese instead. Or swans."

"They don't *kill* them," she said. Rolled her eyes. And departed.

"It's true," conceded Ardis. "But having your feathers plucked off you while you're still alive isn't a walk in the park either."

JASON HAD JOINED the local chapter of a birding group. There he'd met an older lady, a widow who seemed to like him back. He believed she might be his raven.

"How old *is* she?" asked Sarah, blunt as always.

Jason was young, though he didn't look it.

"She's fifty-two."

"If she's, um, your raven," said Sarah. "I mean. Is it a problem that you couldn't have children?"

"Jesus," said Gil, uncomfortable. "Kind of a personal question."

"But that's OK, isn't it? Since we're *people*," said Sarah.

"I don't *want* children. This country isn't safe for birds or men."

"Well said."

"I read it in a magazine. And anyways she already has one. Grown up. His name is Steve. He's a tax accountant. He lives in Sierra Vista."

Maybe Gil could volunteer for the bird group next, suggested Jason.

They needed people to help with surveys. In the national forests and some grasslands and riparian areas. To go around counting the populations of rare birds.

Then he and Gil could volunteer together again, he said, excited.

Gil had to admit—it wasn't a bad idea.

IN BED HE ASKED SARAH if she had wanted kids.

"I wasn't sure, back then," she said, a little dreamily. "The marriage was on a shaky footing. And now I'm too old. The window has closed, I guess."

"You're not *that* old. You could still adopt."

He hadn't planned to say this. But as he did he realized he had been thinking about it. How his mother had been an orphan.

She turned on her side to face him.

"I could?"

"Well. Hypothetically."

"I guess I could," she said.

They lay there. Beneath the bedside lamp on the table next to her he let his eyes dwell on her cat-eye reading glasses. A medical journal splayed open, upside down.

It was odd, but he didn't feel awkward.

"It's not easy," she said. "Foreign adoptions are pretty much off the table now. For the private domestic ones you have to audition. A colleague of mine went through it. They make a brochure for you! Pictures of you smiling and pursuing hobbies in your home and garden. You have to gather testimonials. To your emotional fitness for parenthood. From your family and friends. Then the expectant mother gets to thumb through a sheaf of those brochures. Dozens. Hundreds. Decide if you're worthy. It can take years. And single adoptive mothers? Major handicap. Doctor or not, I'd never get picked. Unless I went for an older child. Public adoption. And started by fostering. Which—I don't know if I'd be a good candidate for that. With my particular career."

"As far as the private adoptions go. You wouldn't have to be single," said Gil.

"Is that so."

"You could have a partner who was unemployed. Able to stay home with the child. Just hypothetically."

"I'd still need a leave of absence, though. I'd want one. If someone trusted me with her baby."

"Well, sure. But then you could go back to work. When you were ready for it."

"Hmm," said Sarah. And smiled.

HADLEY CALLED EARLY on a Tuesday for their regular check-in. He said he'd be announcing his retirement at Christmas. Time to slow down. Spend his weekends angling. He had a fishing shack beside a stream in the Catskills.

Gil had expected it, but still felt nostalgic.

"Well. I'm really going to miss you," he said.

His grandmother would not have approved of this. In her book it would qualify as an emotional outpouring.

In the letter she left for him with the trustees, she'd told him not to address Hadley by his first name. It was purely a business relationship. Boundaries, she counseled, were very important.

He hadn't meant to take the advice, but somehow Hadley had always stayed Hadley.

As Van Alsten had always stayed Van Alsten.

"I have a few candidates for you. Among the junior associates. You've met some of them."

"I only get a *junior* associate? What, I'm not one of your richest?"

Sometimes, talking to Hadley, he had an inane thought and let it come right out of his mouth. Hadley was used to this. He didn't bother to produce a chortle.

"The other senior associates are fossils too. All headed for retirement in the next two years. I don't want you to get passed around like a debutante at a ball."

"Me neither."

"I'll walk you through their profiles soon," said Hadley. "Just wanted to give you fair warning."

"Well, thank you."

"One other matter, before we move on to your year-end giving," said Hadley. "I had to stop the payments to your drunk driver friend. You'll see it reflected on your statement."

"Stopped? Why?"

"Deceased."

Gil took a minute. A slide show played in his head.

Dag microwaving burritos.

Watching cockroaches the size of thumbs scurry around a dirty toilet.

Dag dying.

"You're going to say I told you so," he said.

"He didn't OD, actually. I called that one wrong. No narcotic use. Only a lot of alcohol and tobacco. Also high-risk vices, mind you. For a man in his condition. It was related to his lupus, they told me. Cardiac arrest."

"Oh."

Sober as a judge, Dag had said.

Gil guessed it had been true, technically. Even Supreme Court justices weren't known for their history of sobriety anymore.

"You paid for the funeral," said Hadley.

After they hung up he was disoriented.

Dag had never caught a break. It was tough luck to die so soon after your long-awaited ship came in.

A ship you'd worked so hard to bring.

There was the ship of dreams, moving into the harbor over a blue ocean. Laden with provisions. Full sails billowing out. While fleecy clouds scudded.

Abruptly it ran aground.

SARAH LEFT SOME ADOPTION agencies' glossy flyers on the counter in the kitchen. He read them.

Halloween was her favorite holiday, she said. She always dressed up to give out candy. This year she was going to be a bat. A flying fox, with a padded, fuzzy stomach. There was a nurse at the hospital who sewed a lot. Liked to make costumes for other staff. Took commissions.

Sarah offered to get a bat outfit for him too.

He hadn't worn a costume since he was a boy. Lane had occasionally dressed up for a Halloween party they were going to, but she'd never encouraged him. "Just go as yourself," she'd said. "That's costume enough."

He'd suspected she wanted a straight man to play off of. Looking uptight. Socially reticent.

Or maybe it would have embarrassed her to see him dressed up.

"Two bats, huh?"

"A couple of furry, middle-aged bats."

THE NEIGHBORHOOD HAD A reputation as a trick-or-treating bonanza: some residents gave out handfuls of full-sized candy bars. Groups of children were driven in by their parents from other neighborhoods to gather the spoils.

Some of them ran fast between houses, emitting harsh rallying cries.

Their lust for candy was intimidating, said Sarah from behind her bat snout.

Gil was having trouble with his mask. A whole head, actually. It went on like a hood and was quite realistic, with small, pointed ears on top—a flying fox had surprisingly small ears, for a bat—

and a snout that stuck out. Like a fox's. Hence the name, he guessed.

But it restricted both breathing and sight. He had almost no peripheral vision.

Also, he felt hot beneath the thick fabric and large wings.

Clem and Tom were making the rounds separately, both with their own pack of friends. She was headed to a party afterward, so she came by early.

Her friends were also in black, skintight clothes. Wearing bright-red lipstick.

Wasn't clear what they were dressed as.

"Vampires?" guessed Gil after they left.

"But they had no fangs," said Sarah.

"Robert Palmer girls?" said Gil.

"Gil! You're so eighties. In the pop culture wars, *Star Trek* lost. *Star Wars* won. Robert Palmer's more of a *Star Trek* situation. No retro-cool at all. They haven't heard of him."

When Tom showed up, carrying a plastic jack-o'-lantern full of loot, he was accompanied by an inflatable hot dog and a shaggy gray thing that looked like a mound of hair.

Ardis waved from the curb. She was with the other kids' parents, talking.

"Yeti," said the shaggy mound, when Sarah inquired. "Trick or treat."

"Trick, then," said Sarah.

The pirate, hot dog, and yeti stood there.

"We don't *know* any tricks," said the pirate. Plaintive.

"I know a *joke*," offered the hot dog. "I can tell it."

"OK," said Gil.

"Knock knock."

"Who's—"

"The interrupting hot dog!"

"Ha *ha*," said Gil.

"What are you, some kind of giant rat?" asked the yeti.

"Say *what?*" Gil stretched out his arms. "Does a giant rat have wings?"

"I *still* don't know what you are," said the hot dog, challenging.

"A bat," said the pirate, rolling his eyes. *"Obviously."*

"Flying foxes," said Sarah. "They live in Australia."

"I been there," said the yeti. And shrugged. "It's not all *that*. Just dusty and hot. Like here."

"Can we have candy now?" asked the hot dog.

"A person asks for a little conversation. What's Halloween coming to," Sarah said, and handed it out.

MUCH LATER, AROUND TEN, a lone boy showed up. He had a green face and an elongated forehead under a fringe of black wig.

They'd thought the trick-or-treating was over, so they'd removed their bat heads. Sarah had stripped off her whole costume. Scrubs on underneath.

Gil hadn't gotten around to it.

They were drinking their nightly cocktail.

Sarah opened the door, Gil shuffling after with their bowl of treats.

Frankenstein had no friends. But a few yards behind him, down the front walk, was an adult. A man.

Talking on his cell phone, half turned away.

Him Gil recognized. The angry drunk.

So the Frankenstein monster was Brad.

"Trick or treat," he said.

"Nice scar," said Sarah. "Quite authentic."

Brad/Frankenstein shrugged and held out a plastic bag. Sarah dropped candy into it.

"Thanks," said Brad.

Then he caught sight of Gil. Hard to read his expression under the green makeup. He turned to leave.

"Hey, hi," called Gil.

Brad froze, but the dad looked up.

"I'm Gil. I think we met before. Didn't we?"

Brad was still closer to Gil than the dad.

"Don't tell him," he whispered, his head down. Urgent. Even panicked. *"Please* don't. What I did on the bus. Only my mom knows. *Please.* I promise, I was already punished."

The man was walking slowly toward them.

Captured by Brad's fear, Gil felt a rush of panic himself. Gave Brad a small, quick nod.

"Don't think so," said the man. Shifted the cell phone to his left hand and held out his right one for a shake. "Gary."

"Yeah. We did meet," said Gil. "At the party?"

"Oh right. That housewarming thing? Next door?"

"No. After that. A party here."

"Don't think I made it to that one," said Gary.

"No, you were there," said Sarah. Cheerful. But pushing back. *"I* remember you, too."

"Must have been someone else," said Gary, and smiled thinly.

His voice betrayed no strain. "No worries. Happens all the time. Folks think they recognize me. I've just got one of those faces. Come on, kid. We're done now. You got enough candy. You can pig out. Time to head back."

"His kid's afraid of him," said Gil.

When Sarah had shut the door behind them.

"For sure. Flinched when you called out to him," said Sarah. "And the dad lied right to our faces. He took a quick sip from a flask. When he got off his phone. I mean, we're drinking too. But he was hiding it."

"OK," said Gil. "Wait."

There'd been a sharp buzz of malevolence to the father. A vibration of danger.

"Where's my head? Quick! I need the bat head."

"What? Here," said Sarah, and picked it up. "Wait. Stand still."

She put it on him. Fastened the small toggles at the neck—to do it yourself, best to be in front of a mirror.

"What are you *doing*?" she asked.

"A bit of outreach," he said.

And rushed out the door.

He could have used his night-vision goggles, he thought. They wouldn't have gone on, though, over the bat head.

Streetlamps made scoops of light on the asphalt, but between them it was dark. Most of the houses' porch lights had already been turned off. The jack-o'-lanterns extinguished.

At the sidewalk he looked around: there they were. Two figures receding down the middle of the street.

He followed. With the head on, the bat costume gave him cover.

He gained on them—ahead, the dad was talking on his phone. It gave off its own small light. Brad trailed behind, maybe ten feet or so.

His white bag of candy dangled from a wrist, hitting against one leg as he walked.

Hit-hit. Hit-hit.

He was close. On the phone, the dad seemed to be arguing. Distracted. Swearing.

"Brad!" he whispered.

The boy pulled up short, startled.

"It's OK," hissed Gil. "Just keep walking."

Brad hesitated, then complied, shooting a look forward. On his heels, Gil leaned in.

"I'm keeping your secret. But if you have any trouble," he whispered, "you can always come to me. Or to the glass house. If you ever need help. Will you do that? Nod twice for yes. Will you?"

Frankenstein nodded once. After a second, nodded again.

"OK," said Gil. "Good."

He stopped and let them pull ahead.

Then faded back into the dark.

As bats did.

ONE MORNING HE FOUND a nest in a palo verde tree in the backyard, whose branches hung over the terrace. Inside there was a single egg.

He thought at first it might be a cactus wren's, but of course they didn't nest in November. Hardly any birds did, in the Northern Hemisphere.

Jason said it had to be an old nest. An old egg.

But Gil was sure it was new.

I guess a bird could get confused, said Jason. With the seasons different now. From how they used to be.

ELECTION DAY was upon them. Gil was worried. He wanted it to be over.

Only a midterm, but still.

Ardis had invited them over to watch the returns. She was optimistic. Had hung red, white, and blue streamers in the living room.

Ted seemed less enthusiastic. He'd been subdued for a week or two.

Sarah was coming late from work, so he texted Ted to ask him over for a quick drink on his way home. *Just to lift a glass before we have to join the fray*, he wrote.

Ted didn't text back but appeared at the front door at six on the dot, holding a bottle of whiskey.

"Time I contributed to your inventory," he said.

He looked tired, Gil thought.

He drank his first whiskey fast, so Gil offered him a beer back.

"How's it going?" he asked. They sat at the living-room bar. "I haven't seen you that much."

Ted shrugged and quaffed. In the background the TV was playing election news. The pundits were killing time.

"Enh. I've been better, I guess."

"What's up? Work stress?"

Ted hesitated, then smiled weakly. "May as well say it. She

might not want me to. But I will anyway. Between you and me. Ardis *was* sleeping with someone else."

Gil performed a small, basic calculation. He wasn't supposed to know, clearly.

"Damn," he said.

"She ended it," said Ted. "Guy she met at a conference. Another shrink."

"I'm sorry. That's—well. I'm sorry."

"An adulterous shrink," said Ted.

"Two of them. Technically."

"He's a life-coach type counselor. She doesn't even respect him. Professionally."

"Life coach. Huh."

"What does he coach his clients to do? Screw around on their husbands?"

"In select cases?"

Ted stared into his beer. TV colors reflecting off the neck and shoulders of the brown bottle. They both looked at the beer.

Eye contact was not desirable, Gil realized.

That was OK.

"Back then she was so disappointed in me. That thing with the dancer. I was a cliché. She'd thought I was different. So at the time I kind of gave her permission. For the future. One cheating credit. A get-out-of-jail-free card. I mean, lighthearted. But I still said it. She never used it. Till now."

"A credit?"

"What can I say, we were young. Simple-minded. It took *years* before she trusted me again. Now I know what that feels like. Distrust. Disappointment."

"Sure. Yes."

"It's childish, but I didn't *want* to know what it felt like. I didn't want to have to forgive her. The way she did me. She could have left. Some women would. Most, possibly. But she chose not to."

"She chose right, it seems to me," said Gil.

"This is a test. Not of whether I'll leave. I mean, I'm not leaving. Not a snowball's chance in hell."

"Good," said Gil.

"It's a test of my character. I'm not saying that's why she did it. It was about her, not me. But on my side, what I'm left with, it's a test."

He finished the beer. Gil got up and went behind the bar, poured him another whiskey.

"Thanks, man. I'll go easier on that one. And thanks for listening. I should tell it to a therapist. Ardis fills those shoes, usually. Pro bono. But not this time."

"Talk all you like."

"I guess what I always thought was, she was better than me. That she didn't *need* that kind of selfish freedom. Because we all want novelty. It hits us, from time to time. And I let myself believe that novelty was easier for her to give up on. You know, that dream we all have. That, in the turn of a second, no matter what, we can act on an impulse. Because we're personally free."

They sat nursing their drinks.

Free, Gil thought. Personally free.

Night had fallen while they sat, and his rooms were unlit. Beyond the castle walls, over at the glass house, there was light.

He couldn't see it directly, but he saw its traces. Across his back terrace, beams fell and shadows interrupted.

"It's a basic test," said Ted. "Whether you grab your weapons. Because you feel threatened. Or can lay down your arms after someone has injured you. Just put them down and walk forward. Holding up your white flag."

Surrender, thought Gil.

Maybe it wasn't the coward's way after all. Maybe surrender, when it was called for, was the hard part. Not the fight.

But how did you know when it was called for?

And freedom, that sacred cow that was always invoked as an excuse for bad behavior, all manner of atrocity—what was it, even?

They told you to love it, in the schools and the songs, but never said what it was.

Possibly, to many of them, all it meant was the right to have money. Or get more of it.

So then rich people were always free, as Hadley had once said. Even if, to someone like him, it didn't feel that much like freedom.

And no one else was ever free. At all.

"We better head over," said Ted. "The returns are starting to come in."

"You go on ahead," said Gil. "I'll follow. In a few minutes."

After Ted went out the back door he stayed sitting. He was reluctant to watch the returns. Feared them.

With his own so-called freedom, he'd only ever done what everyone else did. And fed and clothed himself. For a while, also fed and clothed someone else.

As it turned out, a disinterested party.

What *would* he do, if he could unleash his freedom perfectly?

Petty mischief, maybe. He could roam the sidewalks of Phoenix tearing out No Parking signs. Remove all the jarring reminders of a truck's impact on bodies. Of how a few short seconds had turned the world sad. For his grandmother and for him.

One man's freedom would be a city's chaos. After a while, he might begin to coast. Untethered and forgetting.

Return to the comfort of his imagined mother love.

Of course, they'd put the signs up again.

You can't change the facts, Gilbert, his grandmother had told him. All you can change is how you behave. In the face of them.

And possibly how you feel, she'd added gently.

It was a fleeting soft moment.

Freedom can only be found in the mind, my dear, she said. Not in the world.

Unbidden, a picture came to him. Four cardboard boxes. She'd referred to them once or twice. A few belongings of his parents'. Miscellaneous objects. Some were from his father's boyhood, while others had been his mother and father's both. When they were married and had him.

She'd always said they were in "deep storage." What that had meant, he hadn't been certain.

Far away, he'd thought. Under the earth with other treasures. Hidden in secret forever, like in the vast warehouse he'd seen in *Raiders of the Lost Ark*.

When he was getting ready to go off to college, he'd found the boxes.

"Deep storage" meant the attic, as it happened. Marked *James and Emily* 1 through 4.

For his grandmother, he'd understood, it had been too hard to look at them.

He'd opened the first box. Found a model airplane made of balsa wood, with one wing crushed. It was painted blue, with the imprecise brushstrokes of a child, and had a sticker of a white star on the side.

There were two popsicle sticks fashioned into a cross, with bright yarn wrapped around them in stripes to make a diamond. He'd remembered making such items once himself—a craft activity in school.

God's Eyes, the teacher had called them.

There was a booklet called *Three Hundred Brain Teasers: How Many Can You Answer?* He remembered the cover: pictures of a teepee, the Statue of Liberty, George Washington, a thistle, and a witch on a broomstick flying across a full moon.

Back then he'd closed the box again. Felt overwhelmed. And at the same time, distant.

But they'd always traveled with him. Now they were stacked up on a high shelf in his garage. Where the movers had put them.

He would open them all. Tomorrow. It was time: the treasures would be unearthed.

Their contents would replace the signs. Dislodge them.

He was sure of it.

HE DECIDED TO GO A roundabout way, walking over. A tactic of delay.

There was a public path between the wash and the street, on

the other side of Ardis and Ted's backyard. He'd go up it and around. Miss more of the election anxiety.

He walked across his own yard, stepped through the gate onto the softer sand of the wash. It was dark. The air was mild. He was comfortable, though he wore only a T-shirt and jeans.

He hadn't brought a flashlight or his phone. There were spiny plants growing on all sides, but he knew this part of the terrain. Knew the gaps among cactus. On rare nights you could make out the blur of the Milky Way, but not tonight. He could see the rectangle of the TV screen in the glass living room, large and bright.

He heard no sound except the wind moving the trees. A great-horned might be on the wing in the trees behind him. They were silent fliers.

Some of the birds were hunting while others slept. And somewhere, across the globe, still others were making epic journeys in the currents overhead. Their bodies cleverly metamorphosed for the long flight.

If we could only see them, Jason had once told him, in the night skies in their millions.

It would be the greatest spectacle of all.

He stood out in the desert and gazed at the TV screen. It was too far to see the numbers in the boxes. He saw the shapes of maps. Fields of blue and red and the colors of flesh: the faces of the newscasters. The faces of the candidates.

In the wide night around him, their digital images appeared to be the only movement.

Digital faces moved everywhere. Projections that captured so much attention.

Real people didn't move much, though. They stayed on trajectories. Believed in ghosts and God, both quite invisible.

But danger, danger and the need for movement, the need for action, those they didn't see. Refused to believe in.

He *did* believe. But still he went along. Performing small tasks. Planning his own minor life. As though there was no emergency in sight.

If only the birds would take up the fight. Help us, he said, to the sleeping flocks as well as those that were flying.

Your sky is emptying. Mine too.

No help seems to be coming.

But face it. Birds were useless in politics.

In the quiet, by yourself, you could let your thoughts roam. Villains and heroes. Bravery and sacrifice. You could conjure up anything.

He walked to the far edge of Ardis and Ted's backyard, turned and headed up the long path toward the street. He seldom used the path. Less familiar territory. Bushes and cactus on either side.

On his left, behind the bushes, was Ardis and Ted's wrought-iron fence.

He heard voices. Women's. Saw two silhouettes against the light of a streetlamp. Holding wineglasses whose yellow contents caught the light.

Sarah. And Ardis.

Instinctively he took a step back. Hidden by shrubs. He'd retreat, go back around. Give them their privacy.

Then they stepped closer. On the side of the house. Darker but nearer. He hesitated. Eager to get away.

But no longer sure if he could make his escape unnoticed.

"Even that you told *me*," said Sarah, "is kind of too much. Now *I* have to think about it."

"I wanted to be honest. At least with somebody."

"But I'm not just somebody. I'm his *partner*."

"And my best friend."

"I *know*, Ardis. But still. It's a burden. And now I have to carry it."

"I'm . . . OK. You're right, of course. And I'm sorry."

"Sometimes you have to forfeit honesty," said Sarah. More forceful than usual. "For the sake of kindness. I can't believe you don't know this."

Words too faint to hear. Ardis was speaking quietly, and some of her words dropped away.

". . . there'll always be space between Ted and me. Because I only told him part of the story."

"There'd be *more* space if you told him the rest. A lot more. It could sour your whole marriage. All of this. I don't know about you, but I *like* how it is."

Gil's stomach clutched.

". . . do too, but . . ."

"And what would it get you?" Sarah was angry. "Relief? Because you *talked* about it? Some bullshit therapeutic *relief*?"

"It's not that simple, though."

If he stepped out now, they'd definitely see him.

"It *is* that simple. I'm with Gil, you're with Ted. So you have some feelings for the wrong guy. Big deal. Life isn't all therapy sessions, Ardis. Some days it's triage. *My* specialty. This is one of those days. I promise. And what you do next is, you live with it. Every desire that passes through you doesn't have to be exposed.

That's only honesty on the couch, Ardis. At home, right here, it's more like stripping off your clothes because you happen to *feel* like it. And putting that burden on the people who love you."

His chest was being crushed. He made himself take a deep breath.

Val Alsten had told him to breathe, way back then. Take a deep breath, he had said.

The warm feel of his hand on Gil's arm. It came back to him. As if the hand were still there.

"So don't rope Ted in too. He's still recovering from your trivial affair. Your little distraction. Enough already. And sure, there's selfishness here, because I'd also be harmed. If Ted knew. If it turned *ambient*. So would Gil. And even the kids. A ripple effect. We're all—what did you call it? *Enmeshed*. Just let sleeping dogs lie, Ardis."

"—you feel strongly."

"Yes," said Sarah. "Yeah, if you want to keep framing it like a shrink. I *feel strongly* that you'd be wrong to launch a torpedo at your family."

A long pause. Then Ardis sighed.

He could feel tension lift.

"OK," she said. Resigned. "OK, Doc. You're the smart one. You win."

Steps away from him. Toward the sidewalk in front of the house.

". . . think you just wanted *permission*," said Sarah. "Not to tell him. Or even both of them. And I was the only one who could give it to you."

"Maybe you missed your calling. As a shrink."

"Sorry, but no. Hell no."

"And I don't *have* a couch, by the way. I'm not an *analyst*."

The voices diminished. Then he heard laughter. A light laughter. Not carefree. But moderating.

He hadn't known anything. Now he did.

He felt a rush of conceit. Ego, struck through with pride. That Ardis could feel that way about him.

Then he thought of Ted and Sarah, and the pride flipped over. Turned to shame.

Only the pity of it left.

We all want novelty, Ted had said.

She would let go of it. Whatever it was. Order would be restored.

Wouldn't it?

It would. Sarah had seen to it. Sarah was keeping them safe.

The whole of them, he thought. Not just one.

He would hate to see Ted hurt. Or resenting him. The ugliness. And the waste.

He was swaying a bit—had he drunk too much in that short time back at the house?—so he let his arm swing back, meaning to grip the vertical rail of the fence, get steady and push himself off.

But the arm met with pain, up and down, all over. Sharp and hard. In his back, too, and his side, the flesh where his back met his underarm. A searing pain. Overwhelming.

He was halfway into a cactus. He was stuck on a cholla. He knew all about it: the spines had barbs on them.

Jumping cholla, they called it. Propagated itself that way. Segments fell onto the ground and planted themselves.

He pulled his arm forward again: they detached from their bush.

Dozens of their pieces were lodged in him. Piercing.

HE COULD BARELY NAVIGATE through the agony, pangs shooting through his body, but he made himself walk down into the wash again. They couldn't know he'd been a witness.

Not only because it had been low of him, hiding. But also, because to let them know would damage them.

Disrupt their strategy of secrets.

He hardly noticed his surroundings, moving through the underbrush. Barely saw where he was going. Pain distracted him. Tears blurred his vision, in the already-dim.

It felt like a death march through hostile territory. Unbearable. But it had to be borne.

So he had no warning. Almost bumped into him. Thought he was seeing himself, for a bedazzled few seconds. A figment from the mirror—black cyborg.

But no. It was a man with binoculars much like his. A flak vest, or something. Pockets in it. Camo.

Holding a long gun.

Smelling of sweat and whiskey.

Or, no. Tequila, maybe.

The man lifted his scope off his face. It sat atop his head, bulbous.

"What the *fuck*," he said. Gave a short, disbelieving chortle. *"Jesus."*

The dad. What was his name? Gary.

"Man, you're fucked up," said Gary. "You're covered in fucking cactus."

Normally, he thought later, he would have been reluctant. Wouldn't have tackled the problem so directly.

But from inside his cloud of pain, his vicious armature of needles, he felt outside himself.

"Listen, Gary. You need to stop shooting my birds," he said.

An entreaty. But also a commandment. Adrenaline coursed through him, along with pain. He was a burning bush.

He stepped closer, and the guy stepped back.

"*Your* birds? They're not *your* birds."

"Well. In a way they are," said Gil.

"You're really fucked up, dude. Shit, look at you! You should be in the ER. You don't know what you're talking about."

"I've been looking for you. Because the birds *are* mine. You know why? Because I give a shit. And they're not yours. Because you *don't*."

"I can shoot whatever I want. State land, asshole. It's quail season."

"Not at night. And you can't shoot raptors, ever. You killed my favorite hawk."

The guy shifted his gun. From one hand to the other.

"Dude, you've got zero proof."

"Right. Because you do it in the dark. Like a coward. You ferret them out with your gear. Kill whatever you find. While they're sleeping. You sneak around and shoot sleeping birds."

"Fuck you."

"And if I have to report it? I'll report it all."

"All? All fucking *what?*"

He had to take a risk. Gamble. Had to.

A wave of pain made his skin rise up in goosebumps. His scalp tingling oddly at the touch of air.

He was afraid, he realized. But didn't care. Rush forward. Blunder. A vector.

"I'll report it *all*. What you do to the birds. We all know. And what you do to your son. We know that too."

The dad said nothing.

In the dark, Gil couldn't see his face.

"Zero proof," he muttered, after a few beats.

"I'm warning you. Stop shooting my birds," said Gil. "And stop the rest of it. Or else."

And then he pushed past. As Gary, stumbling backward, shrank away.

From the burning, talking bush.

OVER THE WASH, half expecting the impact of a load of birdshot in his back, through his yard, he kept going. Then through the shared gate they'd put in.

Till he was standing at the glass house's back door.

With difficulty he raised his good hand, rapped on it.

It was Tom who came running, slid the door open.

"Hi, Gil," he said. Then did a double take. "Gil's got a lot of cactus!" he yelled. "Dad! Help! Gil's got a ton of cholla stuck in him!"

"Stupid," said Gil, shaking his head.

It was a rookie mistake, here in the desert. Running into cholla. Looked foolish.

Ted got up from the sofa, strode over.

"Shit, man," he said. "Wow. Shit. Hardcore." He flipped on the outside lights. Stepped through the door, held Gil's other arm and steered him toward a deck chair.

"I can't sit down," said Gil. "They'll press into me."

"Right. Right. OK. Just stay standing. Let me go get some tools. Stay right there, Gil. I'll bring you some pain pills."

"*So* stupid," repeated Gil.

"I got cholla once," said Tom. "Not *that* much. But it still really hurt."

Gil closed his eyes, holding the arm out. It shook, but the second he let it relax, the cactus touched other cactus. Bit into him harder.

He had to open his eyes again. He was too dizzy to keep them closed.

"It's OK, Gil," said Tom. High-pitched. Concerned. He took Gil's other hand, squeezed it. "It's going to be OK. My dad will get them out."

Then Ardis and Sarah were there.

"Oh my *God*," said Ardis.

"*Gil*," said Sarah. Horrified. "What did you do, fall into it?"

"Leaned in," he said faintly. *Was* that what he said? He was hazy. "I leaned in."

The penalty was richly deserved.

Would he look at Ardis differently now? Betray what he'd overheard?

He tried to fix his half-shut eyes on her face to find out. See how hard it would be.

But his eyes were still watering, and she blurred.

For a while he'd like to keep her blurry.

Soon Sarah was pulling the cactus out of him with pliers and tweezers. She wore gardening gloves to protect her hands, but in the tough mitts her hands were clumsy, she said. Barbs tore at his skin as they were ripped out.

He swallowed a pill Ted put in his hand. Drank some water.

Ardis, collecting discarded cactus into a shoebox with tongs from the kitchen, said something about Urgent Care.

No, said Sarah. Urgent Care was bullshit. And all he'd get there would be someone like her. At best. Or maybe a nurse practitioner. After a terrible period of waiting.

They had to peel off his shirt, once the largest segments were out of it. To get at the spines that were still attached to him, in his armpit and between his ribs. He felt like a child, standing there shirtless in front of everyone. Exposed and hurting, with one arm raised over his head.

The extractions took a long time. Nausea rolled over him. He started to feel he was spinning. Dreamy.

"I didn't tell you," he found himself confessing to Sarah. He had to confess *something*. "I *did* give him money. You didn't want me to. But I did."

"Gave who—? Oh. *Him?*"

"But then he died."

"Who *died?*" asked Ardis.

"He means the drunk driver," said Sarah. She plucked with her pliers as Gil clenched his teeth.

"You didn't want me to," he said. "And then he had a heart attack."

She gave a hard wrench. He gasped. "Sorry. That one was in deep. Pliers aren't my go-to surgical instrument."

"I gave him money. But I didn't like him. Then he died. I never told him. Now I wish I had."

"Told him what?" said Sarah. She dropped the cactus into Ardis's shoebox.

"That I thought he was a jerk."

Ardis laughed.

"Well. You don't fight for yourself," said Sarah, and shrugged. "Only for other people."

"Oh," he said.

He hadn't seen it. Made him want to laugh too. But he was too busy wincing. Even that seemed funny. The wincing was comical.

He was floating. Wincing and floating.

"Don't fight. For self."

Later he'd tell her about Gary.

If he was wrong about the man hurting his son, of course, he'd been very wrong to threaten him. The idea made his stomach hurt.

A parent's nightmare. To be unjustly accused, by inference and rumor, of abuse.

On the other hand, all Gary had said was *zero proof.* Not a response that typically came from innocence.

"Ted. He seems delirious. What was it you gave him?"

"Hydrocodone. Left over. A scrip from that time I broke my ankle. Figured he needed it."

"Not everyone tolerates Vicodin equally," said Sarah.

He'd never had Vicodin before.

Clem had come over. Her face aghast. He wondered why, then looked down where she was looking. At his arm. It was very bloody. Drips and patches of blood.

"I'm sorry," he said to her. "Disgusting."

"That's OK, Gil," said Clem. "It's not your fault." And smiled. Tremulous. But meant to be encouraging.

He smiled back. Or tried to.

"Keep talking, everyone. Say something to distract him," said Ardis.

"I'll tell about the insects," said Tom eagerly. "I just learned some fun facts. *Gil.* Did you know the global biomass of insects is greater than that of humans by orders of *magnitude*? There are at least *ten quintillion* insects on earth, Gil!"

Good news. Maybe the insects would handle it. Since the dinosaurs didn't have it in them.

The insects might be naturals at revolution, with their hive minds. Their brainless, decentralized intelligence.

That was the answer. Insects. Even more ancient than the birds.

A formidable legion.

"Rise up, you insects," he mumbled. "Please. Rise up."

If only they could see what was coming. If a knowledge of the future could be imparted to them. All the terrible predictions.

What might they do with the knowledge?

But there was a language barrier, sadly.

He couldn't tell them. Didn't know how. His hands were tied. And the birds and insects had no hands.

Lustrous feathers and wings. Sculpted talons. Great dark eyes with no whites. In the case of insects, numerous legs.

He thought of legs for a while. So many legs.

Hairy tarantula legs. Butterfly legs. Fly legs, twitching. Centipede legs. Millipede legs. Shudder. Didn't like those. Scorpion legs. Not his favorites either. Beetle legs. Ant legs. Daddy long legs. The legs of caterpillars.

But not enough hands. No hands to write with. Or hold weapons.

And no words at all.

PADS WERE PRESSED onto his arm and ribs. Cool. Damp. Round cotton pads. They stung. Sarah was doing it.

His arm was smooth again. The sharp things were gone.

"Basically, he's high," she said.

HE DOZED FITFULLY ON a couch, his arm and side bandaged, while the rest of them sat in front of the television. Woke up from time to time and gazed at them.

The children weren't watching the election returns. Clem scrolled on her phone, smiling privately. Tom was reading a book—Gil knew it by its colorful cover. A series he'd read over and over about a dyslexic boy who was, in secret, a demigod. Now and then he reached out and scrounged around in a large bowl of popcorn on an end table.

Ardis sat curled up next to Ted, feet tucked beneath her, head tipped onto his shoulder.

Reassuring. Happy. Reminded of her loyalty to Ted—their tie that abided—he could nearly forget her wandering affection. Know her crush for the blip that it was.

A small blip in a long, steady line.

Sarah sat near them but kept coming back and forth to check on him. Once, bringing a hot drink. Another time, tucking a fleecy blanket around his shoulders. Pressing her lips against his cheek.

He was fuzzy, a throb of pain distracting him. But cozy. Secure. So fortunate to be here.

Inside the castle hovered a shadow version of him, alone, watching this full, well-lit house from the other's emptiness. Looking through the glass, he was divided in two. He saw himself with the family around him.

Glad of it. Almost proud.

As a parent might be. He was his own parent.

He'd learned to be alone, walking. And it was still good now and then. For thought. For recognition.

But being alone was also a closed loop. A loop with a slipknot, say. The loop could be small or large, but it always returned to itself.

You had to untie the knot, finally. Open the loop and then everything sank in. And everyone.

Then you could see what was true—that separateness had always been the illusion. A simple trick of flesh.

The world was inside you after that. Because, after all, you were made of two people only at the very last instant.

Before that, of a multiplication so large it couldn't be fathomed. Back and back in time. A tree in a forest of trees, where men grew from apes and birds grew from dinosaurs.

The topmost branches were single cells. And even those cells were not the start, for they drew life from the atmosphere.

The air. And the vapor. Suspended.

It was the fear and loneliness that came in waves that often stopped him from remembering the one thing. The one thing and the greatest thing.

Frustrating: he could only ever see it for a second before he lost sight of it again. Released his grip. Let it slip away into the vague background.

But it had to be held close, the tree.

In the dark, when nothing else was sure, the soaring tree sheltered you. Almost the only thing you had to see before you slept.

How you came not from a couple or a few but from infinity.

So you had no beginning. And you would never end.

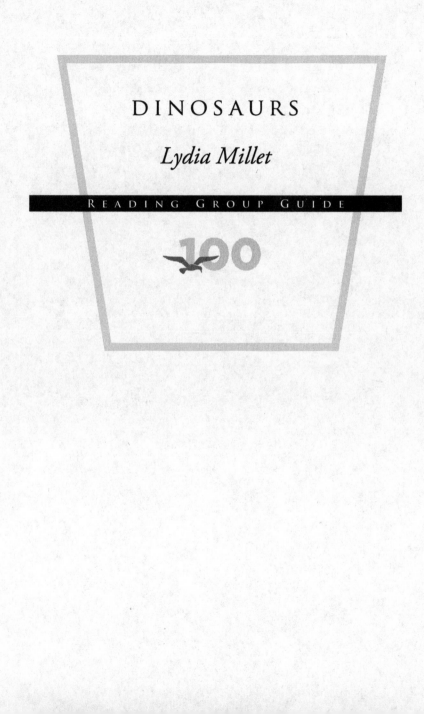

DINOSAURS

Lydia Millet

DINOSAURS

Lydia Millet

DISCUSSION QUESTIONS

1. Lydia Millet's *Dinosaurs* opens with a bird's-eye view of Arizona. What about this perspective on the world captivates Gil? How does the idea of looking at the world from above shape the course of this story? Are there other moments in the novel when something is depicted as though seen from above?

2. "There was something about Ardis. Momentum—you couldn't refuse her. It was easier not to" (p. 13). Does Gil think of his actions in terms of ease and difficulty? Are there other characters who think in these terms? When does Gil refuse someone? What is the significance of refusal for him?

3. Many different visions of freedom come up in *Dinosaurs*. We learn about Gil's youthful dream of giving away all his money, his grandmother's statement that "freedom can only be found in the mind" (p. 214), and Ted's idea of a selfish freedom based on impulses. What is the significance of freedom for Gil? For Ardis and Ted? For Sarah? For Tom? Does *Dinosaurs* arrive at a new understanding of freedom? How would you describe it?

4. What does Sarah mean when she tells Gil, "You don't defend yourself" (p. 161). Do you agree with Sarah? Are there other characters in this book who don't defend themselves? Explain.

5. After discovering Ardis's infidelity, Gil asks, "Why could no one be steadfast? Just stay?" (p. 182) What does Ardis represent to Gil in this moment? Who does he want to be steadfast? How

do concerns about steadfastness and loyalty animate Gil's relationships in this book?

6. Gil describes his walk from New York City to Phoenix saying, "It's not much of a story. It was mostly big roads. Interstates, even. Because to go by the small roads would have taken a lot longer. It went like this: the same, the same, the same. Then for a few miles, slightly different. The same, the same, the same, the same . . . then slightly different. I met some truckers. And saw a lot more roadkill than I ever wanted to" (p. 127). Is this an apt description for *Dinosaurs* itself? Why or why not? What does the walk mean to Gil? What does it symbolize for the story as a whole? Were there other events in the novel that reminded you of Gil's walk?

7. Do you agree with Sarah's decision to intervene on Gil's behalf and tell Dag to stop trying to communicate with him? Gil describes it as "a question of boundaries—they weren't clear. Hadn't been defined. It wasn't her fault. Still, she'd vaulted over one" (p. 162). What are other unspoken boundaries in the novel? How are they protected? How are they transgressed?

8. The slow cycling of weather and seasons in this novel contrasts with the linear development of Gil, Sarah, Ardis, Ted, Tom, Clem, and other characters. What is the significance of time for the plot of *Dinosaurs*? Did you relate to Gil's relationship with time?

9. Birds are ever-present symbols in this book. What does a bird symbolize to you? How did this novel influence your thoughts about birds? Describe the difference between Jason and Gil's relationship to birds in this story. What does this reveal about their personalities?

10. "At a certain point, not to engage is cowardly," Connie tells Gil early in the book, to which Gil replies, "People default to cowardice. At least, *I* do" (p. 51). Do you agree with Gil's

perception about himself and others? At what point in the story is Gil a coward? When is he not? How does this conflict between agency and default responses resonate throughout *Dinosaurs*?

11. When Gil confronts Gary about killing birds at night, Millet writes, "He was afraid, he realized. But he didn't care. Rush forward. Blunder. A vector" (p. 223). Why is it important to know that Gil is afraid? How does fear influence Gil's life?

12. Although this novel is narrated in the third person, Gil's perspective is deeply imbedded in the writing. Why do you think Millet chose the third person? What would be different if the story were written from Gil's first-person perspective?

13. Were you surprised by the relationship between Gil and Sarah? What draws Sarah to Gil? Why is Gil reluctant to breach the boundary between friendships and romantic relationships?

14. Gil remembers learning that all the dinosaurs went extinct sixty-six million years ago and then, in school, discovering that some dinosaurs had survived and that birds are descended from them. How does this knowledge resonate in the plot of the novel? Why do you think this book is called *Dinosaurs*?

15. After reading Dag's email describing how he killed Gil's parents, Gil thinks, "Mother. Mother. Mother. Pain" (p. 160). How did you read this line? What is Dag's role in this story?

16. *Dinosaurs* is an intimate story about a man overcoming trauma and simultaneously a broader story about community, relationships, and the world around us. How does Millet join these parts of her novel? What do these two levels bring out in each other?

17. At the end of the novel, surrounded by his friends in the glass house, Gil has the realization that "he was his own parent" (p. 229). What does this mean? What does Gil do for himself that a parent does for a child? How does this realization allow Gil to be part of the community of people around him?

Meghan Kenny	*The Driest Season*
Nicole Krauss	*The History of Love*
Don Lee	*The Collective*
Amy Liptrot	*The Outrun: A Memoir*
Donna M. Lucey	*Sargent's Women*
Bernard MacLaverty	*Midwinter Break*
Maaza Mengiste	*Beneath the Lion's Gaze*
Claire Messud	*The Burning Girl*
	When the World Was Steady
Liz Moore	*Heft*
	The Unseen World
Neel Mukherjee	*The Lives of Others*
	A State of Freedom
Janice P. Nimura	*Daughters of the Samurai*
Rachel Pearson	*No Apparent Distress*
Richard Powers	*Orfeo*
Kirstin Valdez Quade	*Night at the Fiestas*
Jean Rhys	*Wide Sargasso Sea*
Mary Roach	*Packing for Mars*
Somini Sengupta	*The End of Karma*
Akhil Sharma	*Family Life*
	A Life of Adventure and Delight
Joan Silber	*Fools*
Johanna Skibsrud	*Quartet for the End of Time*
Mark Slouka	*Brewster*
Kate Southwood	*Evensong*
Manil Suri	*The City of Devi*
	The Age of Shiva
Madeleine Thien	*Do Not Say We Have Nothing*
	Dogs at the Perimeter
Vu Tran	*Dragonfish*
Rose Tremain	*The American Lover*
	The Gustav Sonata
Brady Udall	*The Lonely Polygamist*
Brad Watson	*Miss Jane*
Constance Fenimore Woolson	*Miss Grief and Other Stories*